MISSION
UNSTOPPABLE

DAN GUTMAN

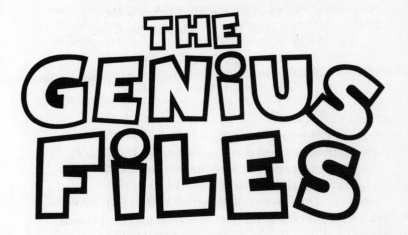

THE GENIUS FILES

MISSION UNSTOPPABLE

HARPER

An Imprint of HarperCollins*Publishers*

Library of Congress Cataloging-in-Publication Data
Gutman, Dan.
    Mission unstoppable / by Dan Gutman. — 1st ed.
        p.   cm. — (The Genius Files ; #1)
    Summary: On a cross-country vacation with their parents,
twins Coke and Pepsi, soon to be thirteen, fend off strange
assassins as they try to come to terms with their being part of a
top-secret government organization known as The Genius Files.
    ISBN 978-0-06-182764-8 (trade bdg.)
    ISBN 978-0-06-182765-5 (lib. bdg.)
    [1. Adventure and adventurers—Fiction. 2. Genius—Fiction. 3.
Brothers and sisters—Fiction. 4. Twins—Fiction. 5. Assassins—
Fiction. 6. Recreational vehicles—Fiction. 7. Family life—
Fiction.] I. Title.
    PZ7.G9846Mn 2011   2010009390
    [Fic]—dc22

Typography by Erin Fitzsimmons
11 12 13 14 15   CG/RRDB   10 9 8 7 6 5 4

First Edition

To Liza Voges

"Do stupid stuff, and even stupider stuff
will happen to you."
—*Nobody said this. But somebody should have.*

Thanks to Edward Cheslek, Robert Jones, Nina Wallace, Lucy Trotta, Jerry Trotta, Linda Clover, and of course Google Maps.

Cont

ents

To the Reader . . .

All the places mentioned in this book are real.

You can visit them. You *should* visit them!

Chapter 1
COKE
AND
PEPSI

There were ten items on Coke McDonald's to-do list on June 17, but JUMP OFF A CLIFF was not one of them.

CLEAN OUT MY LOCKER was on the list.

PICK UP MY YEARBOOK was on the list.

GET BIRTHDAY PRESENT FOR PEP was on the list.

PACK FOR SUMMER VACATION was on the list.

But nothing about jumping off a cliff.

And yet, oddly enough, jumping off a cliff was the *one* thing that Coke McDonald was actually going To Do on June 17.

Not only was he going to jump off a cliff, but first he was going to push his twin sister, Pepsi.

Now, before we get to the cliff-jumping part of the story, maybe I'd better explain something. Why would anyone in their right mind name their children Coke and Pepsi?

It was probably because Dr. Benjamin McDonald and his lovely wife, Bridget, weren't in their right minds when the twins were born almost thirteen years earlier. For one thing, the McDonalds didn't know they would be having twins until after Coke entered the world. The doctors and nurses had pretty much taken off their latex gloves and called it a day when Mrs. McDonald informed them that she felt a funny feeling deep inside—as if she wasn't quite finished. And, lo and behold, she was absolutely right! The doctors and nurses went back to work; and the next thing anybody knew, out popped a bouncing baby girl.

Surprise!

From the start, the McDonalds had decided to name their son Coke. Not because of the soft drink. Because of *coal*. According to Dictionary.com, coke is "the solid product resulting from the destructive distillation of coal in an oven or closed chamber or by imperfect combustion, consisting principally of carbon."

Go ahead and look it up if you don't believe me. I'll wait.

Okay, did you look it up? Good.

Dr. McDonald, a history professor at San Francisco State University, had written a scholarly book about coal's impact on the Industrial Revolution. He always thought Coke would make a good name for a boy. It's short, sweet. It has that hard *K* sound. Like *Kodak. Katmandu. Kalamazoo.*

When Coke's twin sister popped out, Dr. and Mrs. McDonald were faced with a dilemma. Once you name your firstborn son Coke, you can't very well name his twin sister Rachel or Emily or anything too *normal*. It wouldn't sound right.

"How about Pepsi?" one of the attending nurses suggested as a joke. "Coke and Pepsi."

Everyone in the birthing room had a good old laugh over that. But the more the McDonalds thought about it, the more they liked the idea. Coke and Pepsi! It was *perfect*!

Not only that, but it fit their sensibilities. The McDonalds were second-generation hippies from San Francisco who had always disapproved of the rampant commercialization of society. Dr. McDonald was fond of telling his students that the average person living in a city sees up to five thousand advertisements every day. Five thousand ads! What better way to stick it to The Man than to name your kids Coke

and Pepsi? It would be an ironic statement about how corporations control people's lives.

Heck, their last name was already McDonald. Why *not* name the kids Coke and Pepsi?

Naturally, when the local media picked up on the baby names, the Coca-Cola and Pepsi-Cola companies were not happy at first. They made some noises about suing the family. Giving babies the same names as popular soft drinks was an infringement of the companies' copyrights, the lawyers grumbled. (Yeah, as if consumers would confuse the infants with sugary carbonated beverages.)

In the end, the corporate giants decided that kids named Coke and Pepsi would be the best advertising they would ever *have*. And it didn't cost them a dime. This, they agreed, was even better than having kids named Jimmy and Suzy walk around wearing Coke and Pepsi T-shirts.

Of course, growing up with the names Coke and Pepsi can be tough, especially in middle school. Both of the twins encountered a good deal of ribbing when they got to sixth grade, especially Pepsi.

"Hey, soda girl! You're flat!"

But the thing is, no matter how unusual someone's name is, after you hear it a few dozen times, the name starts to fit the person, like a comfortable pair of jeans. You can't imagine that boy or girl ever having a different name. Eventually, kids stopped looking at Pepsi and thinking of high-fructose corn syrup. We humans have a way of adapting to things.

Hardly anybody called her Pepsi, anyway. To most of the kids at West Marin Middle School and just about everybody who knew her, she was Pep. Simply Pep.

Anyway, it could have been worse. The McDonalds could have named the twins Mountain Dew and Sprite. A few years back there was a New Jersey couple who named their son Adolf Hitler. Go ahead and look it up if you don't believe me.

Now *that* kid is going to have issues.

Ordinarily in a story, this is where the author tells the readers what the main character—or, in this case, characters—look like. The author might go on for page after page, painting a glorious word picture of Coke's and Pep's hair, their faces, the way they walk and talk, the way they dress, and so on.

But you know what? Who cares? Do you really care what Coke and Pep look like? Does it really matter to you? It's *boring*. By the time you get to Chapter Three, you will have forgotten the description you read back in Chapter One, anyway. Coke and Pep are twelve-year-old twins, about to turn thirteen in

a week. Okay? Nuff said. That's all you need to know right now.

You really want to know what they look like? Look at the cover of this book. Go ahead, I'll wait.

Okay, now that we got that out of the way, let's move on to the good part—the part where Coke and Pep go over the cliff.

Chapter 2
OVER THE CLIFF

West Marin Middle School sits nestled on a ridge high up in the hills in Point Reyes Station, California. The town's about thirty miles north of San Francisco and very close to Mount Wittenberg, which towers 1,407 feet above the Pacific Ocean. On a clear day, you can be in the school playground and see nearly forty miles. The weather is almost always beautiful. And on this particular day, it was so beautiful that the McDonald twins decided to ditch the school bus and walk home to their house down by the beach. It would be a long hike, but it was downhill all the way.

"I should call Mom and Dad on my cell and tell

them so they won't worry," Pep suggested.

"We'll be home soon," Coke replied. "Don't bother."

The twins talked about their upcoming summer vacation. The whole family would be driving cross-country, all the way to Washington, D.C., where the twins' aunt Judy would be getting married on the Fourth of July.

Neither of the twins was particularly excited about the trip. Sitting in a recreational vehicle for two months wasn't anybody's idea of a good time. They'd have to celebrate their birthday—June 25—in an RV. It was probably going to be the worst summer of their lives, Coke guessed.

The twins hadn't gone far when Pep turned to her brother anxiously.

"Y'know, I have a feeling that somebody's following us," she said quietly.

Both twins turned around to look behind them. Nobody was there.

"Don't be ridiculous," Coke said. "Why would somebody want to follow us?"

"I don't know!" Pep said defensively. "I just have this feeling."

"You and your *feelings*."

Feelings. Like a lot of boys, the whole concept of feelings was lost on Coke. He never understood when people would talk about *feelings*. What are feelings, anyway? You feel something when you *touch* it. When you can hold it in your *hand*. Things exist in the real world, or they don't. Something happens, or it doesn't. According to Coke, there was no such thing as *feelings*.

They had walked a few hundred feet down the road when Pep started to pick up the pace.

"Will you slow *down*?" her brother said, annoyed. "It's not a race. What's the rush?"

"There's somebody behind us," Pep told him. "Don't turn around!"

"Well, how do you expect me to see if there's somebody behind us if I don't turn around?" he replied.

There was indeed somebody behind them, off in the distance. It was a man driving a golf cart. He was wearing a black hat and a black suit.

"See him?" Pep asked.

"So what?" Coke said. "It's a public road. People are allowed on it. He isn't bothering anybody. Maybe he lost a golf ball."

"There's no golf course within *miles* of here!" Pep insisted, walking even faster. "Why is he riding in a golf cart? And why would a golfer wear a suit and tie?"

"Maybe he's disabled," Coke replied. "He needs the

cart to get around."

"And maybe he's a murderer."

"Murderers don't drive golf carts!"

"I'm worried," Pep whispered.

"You're *always* worried."

Which was true. Pep *was* always worried about something. At the least little thing—a hangnail, a creaking sound, a runny nose—Pep would fuss and fret and always expect the worst.

Coke turned his head just enough to conclude that the golf cart was getting closer. He may not have been able to feel feelings himself, but he knew his sister. She was a worrier, but she wasn't paranoid. Sometimes it seemed as though she had a sixth sense about certain things. Coke broke into a slow jog just to be on the safe side, and Pep did the same.

They turned off the road to the left and took the dirt path that went closer to the cliff that lined the road. Common sense said that the guy in the golf cart would stay on the paved road and continue on his merry way.

But common sense wasn't in the cards on this day. When the twins turned around to peek behind them again, they saw that the golf cart had veered onto the dirt path. Somebody was on their tail. He was definitely wearing a black suit, and his hat was one of those old-time bowlers.

"Why is that dude in the bowler hat following us?" Pep asked, a frightened look on her face.

"How should I know?" Coke replied. "Come on, run!"

Their backpacks bopped up and down as they dashed along the edge of the cliff overlooking the Pacific Ocean. The path narrowed, but it was still wide enough for a golf cart to ride on.

The twins ran along the cliff walk until they reached a couple of little wooden shacks. The buildings looked like outhouses, but in fact they were used to store equipment for fighting forest fires.

"Let's hide here," Coke said, pulling Pep behind one of the buildings. "That bowler dude will pass right by."

"And what if he doesn't?" she asked, breathing heavily.

"I didn't take five years of karate for nothing," Coke replied, lifting his right foot. "This is a deadly weapon. I can kill a man with it if I have to. And I know exactly how to do it, too."

Pep remembered the last fight Coke was in, just before he earned his black belt. He'd lost to a kid

who was *blind*. Coke only had one move: a spinning kick that he called the Inflictor. It looked cool but didn't fool anybody. Pep was about to make fun of her brother's lame martial arts skills; but before she could get out a word, a hand clapped tightly over each of their mouths from behind.

"Don't scream," a woman's voice warned. "Your lives are in danger!"

Coke struggled to turn around, but the woman's elbow was pressed against his chest. From the corner of his eye, he could make out that she had dark hair and was dressed in bright red.

"Who are you?" Pep muttered through the fingers clamped to her face.

"My name is Mya," the woman said in an unidentifiable accent. "I am a friend. You need to trust me."

"Why?" Coke said, ripping the hand off his face. "Why should we trust you? You're a complete stranger."

"Because I'm about to save your lives."

"Some dude in a bowler hat is chasing us in a golf cart," Pep told Mya.

"I know."

Mya let the twins go and unzipped the large purse that hung from her shoulder. She reached into the handbag and pulled out a yellow Frisbee.

"You're going to save our lives by throwing a Frisbee at that guy?" Coke said. "You've *got* to be kidding."

"Watch and learn," Mya said.

The golf cart was electric and didn't make much noise, but the twins could hear it crunching along the gravel path as it got closer. Suddenly, Mya leaped out from behind the shed, got into position, and whipped the Frisbee thirty yards down the path. It was almost comical—a woman in a red jumpsuit trying to stop a golf cart with a Frisbee. But nobody was laughing.

A tree branch hung over the path, making it impossible to throw anything in a straight line and hit the golf cart. But apparently Mya had thought of that. She flung the disk in such a way that it skipped off the ground once about ten feet in front of the cart and then rose the rest of the way, striking the cart on its right front tire.

There was a loud *bang* and a plume of smoke; and the front of the golf cart flipped up and backward. Through the smoke the twins could see the man flying out of the cart and over the bushes on the right. The golf cart landed upside down with a *thunk*.

"That was *cool*!" Coke gushed. "What was it?"

"A Frisbee grenade," Mya explained calmly, zipping up her bag once again.

"Where can I get one?" Coke asked.

"They're not for sale."

"Is that bowler dude going to be all right?" Pep asked.

"You don't want him to be all right," Mya replied. "He was trying to kill you."

"Wait a minute," Coke said, still fascinated by the Frisbee grenade. "If that thing had an explosive charge in it, why didn't it explode when it skipped off the ground?"

"It was programmed to detonate upon the *second* impact, not the first," Mya explained.

"But how did you know you were going to skip it off the ground?" Pep asked.

"There's no time for questions now!" Mya barked, pulling open the door to the little shack next to them. "That minor obstacle will only slow them down. Quickly! Take off those backpacks. I need you to put these on!"

She took out two large outfits that looked like over-sized silk pajamas. One was yellow, and the other was red. Both were made of a smooth, synthetic material.

"What is this, bulletproof or something?" asked Pep as Mya handed her the yellow one.

"No, it's a wingsuit," Mya explained. "Quickly! Put it on!"

"Why should we listen to *you*?" Coke asked. "Who

are you, our mother?"

Mya grabbed him around the neck.

"No, but I just saved your lives," she told him. "And I'm going to save you again . . . if you'll let me."

Ever since they were old enough to go outside on their own, the twins had been warned not to talk to strangers. Not to take candy from strangers. Not to get into a stranger's car under *any* circumstances. But nobody ever told them not to put on a wingsuit given to them by a stranger.

Pep threw off her backpack and rushed to stick her feet into the legs of the funny-looking suit. Coke, seeing her, reluctantly took off his backpack, too. He pulled on the red suit and zipped it up in the front.

There was one big difference between these wingsuits and a pair of pajamas: A foot or more of material had been sewn between each elbow and hip, and also between the legs.

"This is ridiculous!" Pep exclaimed. "We're like webbed people."

"I look like Gumby in this thing!" Coke said. "I'm not wearing it."

He started to pull down the zipper at his neck, but Mya stopped him.

"Would you prefer to *die* out here?" she said, looking into his eyes and gripping his hand tightly. "Is that

what you want? These wingsuits will make it possible for you to *fly*!"

"Wait a minute," Pep said. "What are you talking about? Are you suggesting that my brother and I jump off the cliff?"

"It's not a suggestion," Mya said, taking two helmets out of the shed and putting one on each of the twins' heads. "It's the only way for you to survive."

"You gotta be kidding me," Coke said.

"Can't we just call 911?" asked Pep. "They'll be here in a few minutes."

"I don't think you're grasping the seriousness of the situation," Mya told them. "There are people who have no other goal except to kill you."

The twins looked around to see two more golf carts in the distance coming from different directions.

"Look, I'm not jumping off a cliff in some crazy suit just because a strange lady told me to," Coke said. "We'd hit the rocks down there and die. This is insanity."

"You won't hit the rocks," Mya insisted. "As soon as you jump, extend your arms and legs. You will soar like a hawk."

"What about *you*?" Pep asked.

"Who cares about *her*?" Coke yelled at his sister. "Why are you worried about *her*?"

"I'll be fine," Mya assured them. "They're not interested in me. It's *you* they're after."

The golf carts were getting closer. Each one was being driven by a guy wearing a black suit and a black bowler hat. One of the men had a mustache.

"Who are *they*?" Pep asked. "Who's trying to kill us? And why are you interested in helping us? How did you know to come here and wait for us?"

"There's no time to talk now," Mya replied calmly. "All your questions will be answered. But only if you jump *now*. Good-bye. Be safe. Perhaps we will meet again."

She wrapped her arms around both twins and embraced them tightly.

Thwiiiiiiiiiiiiiiiiiiiiiiiiit.

Coke looked up to see a green dart sticking out of Mya's neck. It was inches from his face and probably was intended for him.

Mya's legs buckled, and she crumpled, her eyes rolling back in her head. Coke and Pep caught her before she hit the ground.

"*T . . . G . . . F,*" Mya said, gasping for breath. "*T . . . G . . . F.*"

And then she went completely limp.

"I think she's dead!" Pep shouted.

"Brilliant, Brainiac! Let's blow this pop stand!"

"Where are we gonna go?"

"Where do you think?"

"You mean . . ."

"Yes!"

Coke took his sister's hand and dragged her to the edge of the cliff.

"I can't do this!" Pep yelled.

Coke turned around. The golf carts had stopped about forty yards away. The guys in black suits and bowler hats got out. Both were holding thin tubes about two feet long. They didn't look like flute players, and they sure weren't golfers. The one with the mustache put his tube to his mouth.

"You're gonna have to jump!" Coke hollered to his sister.

"You can't make me!"

"Oh yes, I can!"

With that, he pushed his sister off the cliff.

And then he jumped.

Chapter 3
FLYING

"**A**hhhhhhhhhhhhhhhhhhhhhhhh!"

Chances are you've never fallen off a cliff. If you had, you probably wouldn't be reading this right now. Because you would be dead.

But have you ever jumped off a high diving board? Have you ever dropped into a steep water slide or a half pipe? Have you ever been on a really high roller coaster?

Well, forget it. Falling off a cliff is *nothing* like any of those experiences. You *still* have no idea what the McDonald twins were going through.

When you fall off a cliff, the first forty or fifty feet are a straight vertical drop. The only thing you feel in that first second or two is sheer terror. You can't think about anything else. The good thing is—and this is probably the *only* good thing—you can't worry about your problems. If your parents have been bugging you or some kid at school is hassling you, you don't think about it anymore. If you had an ache or pain in any part of your body, it's gone, instantly.

In fact, you can't think at *all*. You can only experience. It's all sensory. Your nervous system goes into survival mode. Nothing else matters. You may even lose control of your bladder. Luckily, in this case, that didn't happen.

After they tumbled over the edge, the twins spun and twisted and flopped around in the air, screaming their heads off the whole time.

One thought did flash through Coke's brain for a millisecond.

I JUST PUSHED MY SISTER OFF A CLIFF!

What had he done? But he had no choice. If he hadn't pushed Pep and then jumped, he surely would have taken one of those poison darts in the neck, just like that lady Mya did. He had made a snap decision, and he would have to live with it.

Or die with it.

Rocks, ledges, and trees shot past Pep's eyes as she plummeted. Something flashed through her mind, too, for a millisecond.

I WILL NEVER BE NICE TO MY BROTHER AGAIN.

This was the last straw, she thought. She would never again update Coke's iPod for him or help him pick out clothes so he wouldn't look nerdy. Not that it would matter, because they were both about to die.

When you're at an amusement park, no matter how terrifying a ride is, you know you're not going to die at the end. Somebody with an advanced engineering degree carefully designed that thrill ride to simulate weightlessness. You know that thousands of people took that same ride before you did, and they all survived. You know that a safety inspector with a clipboard is required by law to check out the rides regularly. You know that after a minute or two, the ride is going to come to an end. You'll climb out of the little car or whatever and go enjoy some cotton candy.

But when you go flying off a cliff, there are no such assurances. At the end of a free fall, your body will most likely smash into the hard surface of the ground with thousands of pounds of pressure, crushing your flimsy bones. Your internal organs are going to explode like water balloons. Or maybe you'll get dashed against the rocks on the side of the cliff and fracture your skull on the way down. What an

unpleasant way to end a life.

But then again, it would be quick and painless.

At one second into free fall, Coke and Pep were moving about thirty miles per hour straight down. The wind was whipping, ripping past them as they accelerated, pulling at the skin on their cheeks. There was a roar in their ears, like the sound of a jet taking off in their head.

Through squinted eyes, Coke could see Pep below him, flailing her arms and legs, trying to turn herself around. At that point, they were dropping like stones.

By three seconds into free fall, they were close to sixty miles per hour and still picking up speed. Coke had once leafed through a physics book in the library and learned a few facts about falling objects. For instance, any falling body will accelerate until it reaches what is called terminal velocity: for a human, about 120 mph.

But terminal velocity varies depending on the object that's falling. A large, flat object, like a piece of paper, will fall a lot slower than a penny. When the twins stuck out their arms and legs, their rate of descent slowed down.

Suddenly, Coke realized what he was doing. He had seen a YouTube video about something called wing-suit BASE jumping just a few weeks earlier. People jump off cliffs wearing these strange-looking wing-suits, and they can actually *fly*. It blew his mind.

Coke had been intrigued enough to do a Google search of wingsuit BASE jumping. Go ahead and look it up. People actually jump off cliffs for *fun*, and they've been doing it since the 1930s. According to legend, seventy-two of the first seventy-five people who tried it died. Then, in the 1990s, a French skydiver named Patrick de Gayardon developed a wingsuit that worked. Well, it worked some of the time, anyway. He died in 1998 after jumping off a cliff in Hawaii; but other skydivers took up the "sport," and better wing-suits were designed.

Coke realized he didn't have to die. The wingsuit could save him.

At four seconds, Coke remembered what Mya had told them: *Extend your arms and legs. You will soar like a hawk.*

Not to get all scientific on you, but if you throw gravity, acceleration, air resistance, and hundreds of feet of vertical drop into an equation and then you add the fabric of a wingsuit as it rushes against the wind like the wing of an airplane, you begin to get lift. And when you're falling off a cliff, lift is a *very* good thing to have.

When wearing a wingsuit, you can manipulate

23

your flight by changing the angle of attack or the position of your body, or by loosening or tightening the fabric of the wingsuit. A typical skydiver will free-fall 110 to 140 miles per hour. Wearing a wingsuit, you can eventually reduce that to as little as 25 mph.

Coke extended his arms and legs as far as he could, and instantly he felt the air resistance. He was starting to move not just down, but also forward. He felt himself slowing and leveling off, like a glider. The air rushing by caught the fabric between his limbs, and the wingsuit billowed out. His body had been turned into an airfoil.

He looked down and saw that his sister had figured out the same thing.

If you had been standing on the beach on that sunny day and had looked up, you would have seen two almost-teenagers slingshotting over your head, facedown, with their arms and legs wide apart to catch the wind.

They were flying!

From the dawn of time, when the first primitive humans looked up in the sky and saw birds above them, they probably wished they could fly. How glorious it would be to soar overhead. For all our intelligence, our technology, and the progress we've made over the centuries, many of us would be happy to give it all up if we could only become birds.

Being human is great. Nothing beats being at the top of the food chain. Opposable thumbs are handy and all for picking things up. But if only we could *fly*!

Coke took a moment to look around. Below was the beach. To the right, in the distance, he could see his neighborhood.

The cliffs of Point Reyes are more than a thousand feet above the Pacific Ocean. It looks like a long way down when you're standing on the beach looking up. From the other direction, as you're dropping, it doesn't seem that far at all.

Just as Coke and Pep were starting to relax and their heart rates were returning to something approaching normal, both twins had the same terrible thought.

How am I supposed to land?

They were moving almost sixty miles per hour. You wouldn't jump out of car that was moving sixty miles per hour. The wingsuits had no source of power to keep the two of them in the air. Without a source of

power, gravity always wins in the end.

Their eyes widened as they saw objects on the ground getting bigger. There wasn't a lot of time.

Coke looked down. The thing *had* to have a parachute attached to it. In old war movies, skydivers always pulled a rip cord to open their chute.

The ground was coming up fast. Desperately, Coke reached behind him. His hand found some cloth, and he yanked it.

The material gave way, and Coke felt something happening behind him. He turned around to see a huge red canopy unfurling over his head. There was a big jolt when the canopy caught the air; and then as it opened all the way, it yanked at him and slowed him down even further. He saw Pep's yellow chute open just before his did. She was about two hundred feet in front of him.

They weren't flying anymore. They were floating.

"Woooooooooooo-hooooooooooooooo!" Coke shouted.

Somewhere in the back of his brain he remembered hearing the expression "hit the ground running." He knew what it meant: to get started on a project quickly. But now he realized where that expression came from. A parachutist has to hit the ground running. If parachutists don't, they're going to hit the ground hard, probably breaking their legs.

The twins felt themselves touch the sandy beach and ran as if they were being chased by a pack of wild dogs. It felt like they had been in the air for an eternity, but in fact it had been less than ten seconds.

Panting, breathless, Pep forgot what she'd thought about her brother after he pushed her off the cliff. She ran over and hugged him tightly. Then she got down on all fours and kissed the ground.

Chapter 4
HOME SWEET HOME

For a minute or two, the twins knelt in the sand, catching their breath, clearing their heads, and trying to comprehend what had just happened to them. Except for a few seagulls circling overhead, the beach was empty. Nobody had seen them land.

Finally, Coke looked up at the cliffs and marveled that he had jumped from such a great height and survived.

"I *told* you we should've taken the bus," Pep said, panting.

"What fun would that have been?" Coke replied, cackling.

Pep unzipped her wingsuit and peeled it off. There

was a Dumpster down the beach. She crumpled the suit and parachute into a big ball and stuffed them into the Dumpster. Coke did the same. The wingsuits probably cost somebody hundreds of dollars, but neither of the twins ever wanted to see those things again.

Together, Coke and Pep climbed the wooden steps leading off the beach to the main road. Looking around, they knew they were about a mile from home.

"How are we gonna tell Mom and Dad about this?" Pep asked.

"Are you crazy?" Coke replied. "We're not gonna say a *word* to Mom or Dad. You know how they worry. They would never believe it, anyway."

The twins hiked away from the beach, into the hills and along the narrow road until they approached Point Reyes Station. It's a small town in the middle of a national park called Point Reyes National Seashore. Soon they could see their house. There was an RV parked in front with the words *Cruise America* painted on the side.

And there were two figures on the front lawn.

"They're waiting for us," Pep said, groaning.

And so they were. Dr. and Mrs. McDonald had been sitting there on lawn chairs for a while, fretting

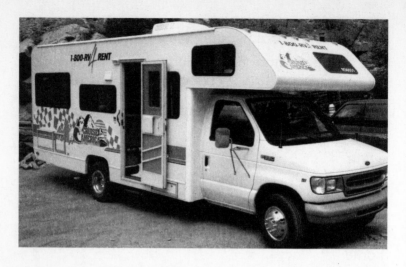

and looking up and down the street with binoculars. When they spotted the twins walking toward them, they jumped up to greet them.

"You're late!" Dr. McDonald hollered. "Why weren't you on the school bus?"

"We decided to walk home," Coke said, hoping that would end the discussion.

"Both of you are a mess!" Mrs. McDonald yelled. "What were you doing: wrestling on the beach? Is that any way to treat your school clothes?"

"We were worried sick," Dr. McDonald went on. "We thought something *terrible* might have happened!"

The twins shot glances at each other. *If they only knew.*

"We're sorry," they said in unison.

It's amazing how a simple, sincere apology will usually melt the hardest of hearts. At least temporarily. Dr. McDonald threw an arm around each of his children and pulled them close.

"Anything exciting happen today?" he asked.

The twins looked at each other again.

"Nah," Coke said. "Same stuff, different day."

"Tell us the truth," their mother said. "Were you two in detention again?"

"No!" Coke replied indignantly. "Don't be ridiculous! We just, uh . . . jumped off the cliff and parachuted home."

"Aha-ha-ha!" Dr. McDonald chortled. "I love you kids!"

"Five more minutes and we were going to call the police to report you as missing, you know," Mrs. McDonald told them. "Where are your backpacks?"

Pep had no answer for that one. They had ditched their backpacks up on the cliff when that Mya lady gave them the wingsuits to wear. Pep looked at her brother, who was a much more skillful liar than she.

"We left 'em at school," Coke said. "We'll get them tomorrow. There was no homework."

"You should have called home," Mrs. McDonald said sternly. "Why do you think we got you cell phones?"

"We . . . forgot," Coke said.

When in doubt, "we forgot" can get you out of just about any mess you got yourself into. It may make you look like an airhead, but that's better than admitting the *real* reason you did the dumb thing you did.

"You'd forget your heads if they weren't screwed onto your necks," Dr. McDonald said.

"Actually, Dad, our heads aren't screwed on," Coke replied. "They're attached with tendons, ligaments, muscles, that sort of thing. If heads were screwed on, it would be a simple matter to do head transplants."

Dr. McDonald shook *his* head: Kids!

He was the kind of man who was organized almost to the point of obsession. Everything in his office was tidy, efficient, labeled, and filed in alphabetical, chronological, or numerical order. He took pride in the fact that he could put his fingers on any piece of paper he needed within seconds. It was inconceivable to him why his children lacked this essential human trait. They must have inherited a scatterbrain gene from their mother, he assumed.

Mrs. McDonald prepared an early dinner while the twins showered and changed their clothes upstairs. Her husband's professional life revolved around the serious study of American history, but her interests were different. Mrs. McDonald was the founder and only employee of *Amazing but True*, a web-based magazine devoted to odd facts and (some would argue) useless information.

Every day, almost a million people clicked on to the site to learn that, for instance, the total surface area of two human lungs would just about fill a tennis court. Or some other piece of trivia. Neither of the McDonald parents made a lot of money, but Mrs. McDonald's income from *Amazing but True* was more than the salary Dr. McDonald earned teaching history at the university. Because of this, when tough family decisions needed to be made, it was usually Mrs. McDonald who called the shots.

She rang the little bell she kept in the kitchen, and the rest of the family charged down from the second floor. Spaghetti was on the table.

Any anger Mrs. McDonald had had about the children coming home late from school was gone. She heaped meatballs on everyone's plates.

"Are you kids excited about our trip?" she asked after they had dug into the food. "We should be somewhere in the Midwest next week for your birthday, and you know we've got to get to Washington, D.C., by July Fourth for Aunt Judy's wedding."

In all the excitement, Coke and Pep had almost forgotten—in two days, after school let out for the summer, they would be leaving for a driving vacation

33

that would take them nearly three thousand miles across the United States and then back.

"I can't wait!" Pep gushed, with just a bit more enthusiasm than was necessary. In fact, she dreaded the trip. At home, there were new clothes that needed to be tried on, texts from her friends that needed to be replied to, videos and TV shows that needed to be watched, and web sites that needed to be surfed.

"It will be good for you kids to see Mount Rushmore, the great national parks, and the Lincoln Memorial," said Dr. McDonald. "All those things you learn about in school but never see with your own eyes."

"Oh, that reminds me!" Mrs. McDonald said. "You'll never believe what I found out today. Do you know what they have in Cawker City, Kansas?"

"What?" everybody said.

"The largest ball of twine in the world!" Mrs. McDonald told the family. "Some guy spent years rolling twine in his garage to create this ball, and now it's *gigantic*. We can go see it on our way east!"

Coke glanced over at Pep to see if she was giggling. Their mom always got excited when she heard about some new oddball place that she could put on *Amazing but True*. Pep avoided making eye contact with her brother, because she knew it would crack her up.

Dr. McDonald just rolled his eyes.

"It's just a silly ball of twine, Bridge!" he said. (He had shortened Bridget to "Bridge" on their first date and had been calling his wife that ever since.)

"It's not just *any* ball of twine, Ben," Mrs. McDonald shot back. "It's the biggest one in the world!"

"It's *twine!*" Dr. McDonald argued, even though he knew from experience that arguing with his wife was a waste of time. "It's not the bloody Grand Canyon. It's not Mount Everest. It's a ball of string!"

"I must see it with my own eyes," she replied simply.

And that was the end of the discussion. Dr. McDonald shook his head. One of the things that attracted him to his wife in the first place was their mutual interest in history. Only later did he realize that she was interested in the history of nonsense. Weird places. Meaningless facts. Strange people. Enormous balls of twine.

Coke knew about the ball of twine in Kansas. In second grade, he had read about it in *Weekly Reader*. He remembered that it was almost nine tons!

I should probably mention here that, in fact, Coke McDonald remembered just about *everything* he had ever seen or experienced. The school psychologist tested him and told Coke he had an eidetic, or photographic, memory. In his mind, he could "see" just about any image he had ever seen with his eyes. In

second grade, Coke had memorized the periodic table of elements, all the way to lawrencium. And he did it without trying.

"Okay, okay, we'll go see the silly ball of twine, if that will make you happy," Dr. McDonald said grumpily.

Coke had a theory to explain grown-ups, as he did for most things in life. In his view, babies are born with a specific number of brain cells, which waste away and die off as people get older. So by the time they reach thirty—and certainly by the time they reach forty—most of their brain cells are gone. This explains why grown-ups do and say the things they do.

To back up his theory, in third grade Coke did a school research project involving music. He made a list of the greatest composers in history, from Beethoven to the Beatles. Then he tracked when they wrote their best music.

Irving Berlin wrote his first hit song—"Alexander's Ragtime Band"—when he was just twenty-three years old. The Beatles made *Sgt Pepper's Lonely Hearts Club Band*, their most innovative album, when John Lennon was twenty-seven and Paul McCartney was twenty-five. Beethoven started going deaf at thirty-one. Mozart was composing minuets at age five and was dead at thirty-five.

Almost as a rule, composers created their finest work in their twenties. There was a severe drop after the age of thirty. This, to Coke, was proof that the human brain deteriorates by the time people become parents. Which explains why parents are so weird. They're essentially operating with an empty skull filled with dead brain cells.

The spaghetti hit the spot. The rest of the dinner conversation was all about the cross-country trip. They would be heading out in two days, after the last day of school.

It was Dr. McDonald's view that all Americans should travel cross-country at least once in their lives.

"You can't see America by flying over it," he told the family. "You've got to hit the open road, breathe in the fresh air, explore the country like the pioneers did. We'll be like a modern-day Lewis and Clark expedition."

"Did Lewis and Clark have an RV?" asked Coke, smirking.

"Maybe we'll be like a modern-day Donner Party," Pep remarked.

"Very funny," said Mrs. McDonald.

The Donner Party consisted of a group of families from Illinois who tried to get to California in 1846.

They got caught in early winter snowstorms, ran out of food, and were forced to resort to cannibalism to survive. Pep found the Donner Party fascinating.

"If we had to eat one of us," she said as she held up a meatball with her fork, "which one of us would you eat?"

"I'd eat Dad," Coke replied. "He weighs the most, so he's got the most meat on him."

"But it's mostly fat," Pep countered. "Mom would be more tender."

"Are you calling me fat?" asked Dr. McDonald.

"That's sick," Mrs. McDonald said. "No Donner Party talk over dinner."

The dishes were cleared away and the table sponged off. Dr. and Mrs. McDonald went upstairs to begin packing for the trip, leaving the twins to load the dishwasher.

"Remember that lady in the red suit we met at the top of the cliff?" Pep asked her brother.

"Yeah," Coke recalled. "Her name was Mya,"

"Do you think she's . . . dead?"

Both twins shuddered at the thought.

"Maybe," Coke said. "I remember what she said right after that dart hit her on the neck—*T-G-F*."

"Oh yeah. What do you think that means?"

"Thank God it's Friday?" Coke guessed.

"Today is Thursday," Pep told him. "It has to mean something else."

"Beats me," he replied. "It's probably nothing. Those bowler dudes in the golf carts probably weren't even after us. Maybe they were trying to get somebody else."

Pep added detergent to the dishwasher and turned it on.

"Y'know," she told her brother, "I don't really want to go cross-country, but now I think this is a good time for us to go on a long trip."

"Why?"

"Because I have the feeling that somebody out there is trying to kill us."

Chapter 5
DR. HERMAN WARSAW AND THE GENIUS FILES

Somebody certainly *was* trying to kill the McDonald twins. And this somebody would prove to be amazingly persistent.

We need to rewind the story a bit here. Back to September 11, 2001. A century from now when kids learn about American history in school, it will probably be divided into everything that happened *before* 9/11 and everything that happened *after* 9/11.

It was on that tragic day that Dr. Herman Warsaw decided to take a cigarette break. This decision would change his life. In fact, this decision would ultimately change a *lot* of lives.

Born in Poland, Dr. Warsaw was a brilliant man,

and one whose brain examined the world differently from the rest of us. As an amateur inventor, he had made a small fortune creating a GPS that people could have implanted under the skin of their dog or cat so that if the pet ran away, it could be tracked down easily.

With the royalties he earned from his invention, Dr. Warsaw didn't have to work for the rest of his life. But he offered his services as a consultant for one dollar a year at the Pentagon in Washington, D.C. America had been good to him. He wanted to give something back.

Dr. Warsaw was an odd-looking sort. He was young at the time—barely thirty—but he had the look of an old man. He wore baggy brown suits and a fedora as if he had stepped out of a 1940s gangster movie. He was rail thin and slightly bent over. He had the squinty-eyed look of a man who spent too much of his short life staring at computer screens instead of interacting with people in the real world.

Smoking two packs of cigarettes a day didn't help any. Oh, Dr. Warsaw had tried to quit. Lots of times. He tried hypnosis and acupuncture and patches and gums and just about every over-the-counter cure-all on the market. But nothing worked. He had to have a cigarette in his hand at all times, even if he wasn't smoking it.

Lucky for *him*. It was the pull of that addiction that made Dr. Warsaw step out of his Pentagon office at 9:38 a.m. on September 11, take the elevator down from the third floor, and walk outside into the parking lot for a quick smoke.

He had just flicked his Bic when the horrible roar of jet engines caused him to jerk his head upward. That sound was *way* too close. Planes weren't permitted to fly anywhere near the airspace above the Pentagon, the Capitol, the White House, or any top-level government building in Washington. But there it was, a plane diving out of the sky and heading toward him.

One second later, American Airlines Flight 77 from Washington Dulles Airport—a Boeing 757—clipped a light pole at 350 miles per hour and slammed into the Pentagon less than fifty yards from where he was standing.

He covered his eyes to shield them from the light and heat. It was terrifying. The plane hit the building with such force that it was literally swallowed up by the Pentagon itself. It entered so cleanly that for years afterward conspiracy theorists were claiming that no plane had even struck the building. They said it had to be an inside job: the government must have purposely set off a bomb.

But Dr. Warsaw knew what happened, because

he saw it with his own eyes. The nose of the plane tore right through his office. If he had been sitting at his desk at that moment, he would have been dead instantly.

A huge fireball erupted, and the Pentagon was in flames. One hundred and twenty-six people in the building died that day, plus sixty-four people on the plane. Less than an hour earlier, two planes had hit the World Trade Center towers in New York City. If there were still any doubts that America was under attack, they were gone. In a few short minutes, history would have to be rewritten.

Dr. Warsaw sank to his knees involuntarily and looked at the cigarette in his hand. His life had been spared. It was at that moment that he made a firm commitment to devote the rest of it to his country.

As the sirens began to wail and the fire trucks pulled up outside the Pentagon, an idea flashed through Dr. Warsaw's brain. It was fleeting, one of those ideas that could have been lost in a moment if he had been distracted. But it was an idea that would change the world.

Dr. Warsaw pulled out the little digital recorder he kept in his pocket just for odd moments like this when inspiration struck. As smoke and flame spewed out of the ruins of the Pentagon, he pushed the RECORD

button and started to make some quick, clipped, verbal notes. . . .

". . . nation under attack . . . multiple problems . . . nation divided . . . unsolvable . . . no agreement . . . society overwhelmed with complexity . . . cannot see forest for trees . . . older generation inflexible, stagnant . . . kids are moldable . . . figure out solutions . . . start over . . . geniuses . . . standardized test scores . . . find them . . ."

These ramblings would have sounded like gibberish to anyone who happened to be listening. But later, Dr. Warsaw would sit down and synthesize his shorthand audio notes into a 434-page manifesto titled "The Only Way Out: The Simple Solution to America's Most Pressing Problems of the 21st Century."

No, you can't find it at Barnes & Noble. Don't bother looking it up on Amazon.com. "The Only Way Out" was a top secret document that was written for, and distributed to, a very small group of government officials.

It would come to be known around Washington as The Genius Files.

It would be impossible to reproduce Dr. Warsaw's entire document here. It would also bore you to tears if you had to read it word for word. But here's the summary on the final page . . .

In conclusion, civilization in the early 21st century is facing multiple serious problems. We've got international terrorism, global climate change, economic meltdown, dependence on unstable oil supplies, a failing education system, senseless wars, loose nukes, insane dictators, drugs, hunger, obesity, cancer, dwindling water and oil supplies, poverty, unemployment, racism, and overpopulation.

Our nation is divided, making these problems seem insolvable. Democrats and Republicans, liberals and conservatives, young and old, North and South, rich and poor can't agree on anything. And that's not even taking into account the various races, ethnic groups, and religions, each with their own worldview and self-interest.

Nothing ever seems to get done to solve these problems. Our society is overwhelmed by the complexity of our situation. The problems are simply too complicated and entrenched for the current generation of leaders. They're paralyzed.

It is time to start over. With children.

In Dr. Warsaw's view, the grown-ups of the world were too set in their ways to change and solve the complex problems they created. The only way to solve the problems would be for the United States government to seek out the smartest young people in the country and enlist them as problem solvers.

"Sometimes you can't fix things," he liked to say. "You have to replace them."

In other words, America would have to start over from scratch with young geniuses. And these geniuses needed to be identified from the earliest age possible in order to cultivate and use their skills over the long term.

How? It would be simple, really. In fact, the mechanism was already in place: the standardized tests routinely given each year to every American child in public school. All that was needed was to pick out the best and the brightest and recruit them to solve the nation's problems.

As you might expect, this revolutionary idea was met with skepticism by the powers that be in Washington. Expecting *kids* to accomplish what the smartest adult minds in the world could not seemed outrageous to many. Some adults were, frankly, threatened by the idea. It would take a few years and a change in presidents for Dr. Warsaw's plan to get approval and funding. It appeared as a tiny earmark in the economic stimulus package that was signed into law in early 2009. And when the disgruntled senators were finished bickering over it, the funding was sliced in half.

But finally, in the spring of 2009, after every child in America had been tested and retested during the school year, a very select group of children were chosen to be the first group of YAGs: Young American Geniuses.

Proud parents all over the country received letters in the mail informing them that their children were among the smartest children in America. These special kids were more than simply "gifted and talented." They would be enrolled in special advanced placement classes and enriched extracurricular activities the next school year. They would be put on the fast track to eventual college scholarships. They were touted as the leaders of tomorrow.

What the parents were *not* told was that their children were being secretly recruited to carry out some of the government's most important—and dangerous—missions. Their kids would be like unmanned drones, assigned to solve the problems that could not be solved by adults.

These children were guinea pigs, and they came

from all over the country. Small towns and big cities. White kids, black kids. It was like the old Armour hot dog jingle: "Big kids, little kids, kids who climb on rocks. Fat kids, skinny kids, even kids with chicken pox."

Kids like Coke and Pep McDonald.

Chapter 6

DETENTION

The McDonald twins didn't know they had been selected to be part of a special program for gifted and talented students. A letter informing their parents of that fact *had* arrived at their house two months earlier, back in April. But unfortunately, Dr. McDonald assumed the letter was just another school fund-raiser and threw it in the trash without opening the envelope.

Now it was June 18, the last day of school, and nobody was paying attention in class. How could you? West Marin Middle School was air-conditioned; but for some mysterious reason, in June, the temperature in half of the classrooms was up over ninety degrees and in the other half you felt as if you were going to school in an igloo.

Early that morning when the teachers arrived at school, one of them found two backpacks labeled MCDONALD leaning against the front door. These were the backpacks that Coke and Pep had abandoned at the top of the cliff the day before. There was no note, no explanation of who had dropped them off. They were returned to the twins during homeroom.

"Later," Jimmy Erdman said to Coke in the hallway after sixth period.

Jimmy Erdman was not part of the YAG program. He wasn't gifted or talented. Far from it. He was barely passing. Jimmy and Coke didn't have a whole lot in common. Jimmy had no interest in books, learning, science, or anything that involved too much thinking. He had little intellectual curiosity. But the two had known each other since first grade.

Most people tend to drift away from their childhood pals as they develop new interests and new friends. But Coke and Jimmy never did. There was a comfort level there. It's easy to trust somebody you've known all your life.

"Later," Coke replied, and headed down the hall to the health room.

The health teacher, Mrs. Audrey Higgins, had that look on her face. It was the look that said she hated her job, she hated her life, and she hated the kids she had to teach. And they hated her right back.

"Today we're going to learn how to brush our teeth, *correctly*," Mrs. Higgins informed the class.

Coke groaned, and Mrs. Higgins probably heard it. He found it inconceivable that sixth graders had to be taught how to brush their teeth or that precious class time would be wasted on something so commonsensical. He looked around to see if anybody else in the class saw the ridiculousness of it all. They just stared back at him blankly. *Zombies*.

Mrs. Higgins was a tall woman with short hair. She squirted a dollop of hand sanitizer, which she always kept on her desk, and rubbed the stuff into her palms. Then she picked up a toothbrush.

"Grasp the handle firmly," Mrs. Higgins told the class, "and always brush up and down. Never side to side."

Coke had no real problem with Mrs. Higgins's tooth-brushing technique. But he did have an interest

in busting chops, especially when it came to grown-ups.

"What's wrong with brushing from side to side, Mrs. Higgins?" he asked politely.

Mrs. Higgins stopped for a moment to look at Coke. She was used to kids like him: bored, supersmart know-it-alls who amused themselves by asking dumb questions.

"If you brush from side to side," she explained slowly, as if he was developmentally challenged, "your teeth will grow in crooked. That should be self-evident, Mr. McDonald."

It also should have been the end of the discussion, but Coke couldn't let it drop.

"Why would they grow in crooked?" Coke asked. "If you put an equal amount of pressure on the teeth as you brush to the left and an equal amount of pressure as you brush to the right, the pressure on both sides would be equal; and the teeth would have no reason to grow in anything but straight. Unless, of course, you're claiming that Newton's third law of motion is incorrect. That is, for every action, there is an equal and opposite reaction."

A few of the boys in the back snickered. They had no idea what Coke was talking about, but they could tell he was giving Mrs. Higgins a hard time. She looked at Coke wearily. She'd had enough of him and his attention-getting devices.

"That's detention for you, McDonald."

"What?" Coke shouted. "What did I do? You're gonna give me detention because I questioned you about how to brush *teeth*? Are you kidding me? It's the last day of school! I was just exercising my freedom of speech."

"Your freedom of speech ends at my ears," Mrs. Higgins said.

"This is child abuse; that's what it is!"

She ignored him. The bell rang, and everybody pushed through the front door chanting the chorus of Alice Cooper's "School's Out." Coke trudged to the detention room.

It was a depressing, windowless room in the basement of the school. On the whiteboard, somebody had scrawled: PAY ATTENTION AND AVOID DETENTION. Coke was surprised to see one other student in the room, sitting in the second row: his sister.

"What are you in for?" she asked Coke. "Armed robbery?"

"I questioned the philosophy behind Mrs. Higgins's tooth-brushing technique," he replied. "And you?"

"Chewing gum," Pep said.

"Nice move," Coke said. "Got a piece for me?"

Pep opened her mouth to show him the only piece of gum she had.

It just might be a long afternoon. Coke took a seat and opened his dog-eared copy of *The Catcher in the Rye*. He hadn't read a children's book since first grade when he decided they were too easy.

"This is totally unfair," Pep complained. "What kind of teacher gives detention on the last day of school? We're probably the only ones left in the whole building. Everybody else is gone for the summer."

A minute later, Mrs. Higgins came into the room. She was wearing white gloves. All the West Marin Middle School kids knew that Mrs. Higgins was germ phobic and obsessive-compulsive about personal hygiene. That was probably why she became a health teacher in the first place. When she was feeling particularly paranoid, Mrs. Higgins would put on her gloves. Kids would make fun of her behind her back.

When she saw Pep and Coke sitting there, she smirked. Coke refused to give her the satisfaction of eye contact.

"How long will this be?" Pep asked Mrs. Higgins.

"As long as it takes," the teacher replied.

Pep slumped in her seat and looked at the door. It was wooden, with a thin sliver of window in it just a few inches wide. The school janitor, Mr. Rochford, walked by pushing a broom. He glanced inside as he passed.

Mr. Rochford was a creepy-looking, extremely obese man with a big, bushy beard and mustache. As far as the students knew, he had never said a word to anybody, which led to all sorts of speculations and rumors about him. Some said he was ashamed because he couldn't speak English. Others insisted he was a deaf mute. The conspiracy crowd claimed he had his tongue ripped while serving time in a Bolivian prison. Everybody called him Bones because he was so fat.

Her cell phone rang, and Mrs. Higgins rushed to open her pocketbook. She said hello on the third ring, but the call was dropped.

"Excuse me," she said. "I'll be back."

Mrs. Higgins went out into the hallway. The door closed behind her.

Coke thought briefly about just picking up and walking out of there. What could Mrs. Higgins do, suspend him? It was the last day of school.

But then the lock on the door clicked. There was no escape.

"What do you think janitors do over the summer?" Pep asked her brother. She had a way of caring about people in whom most other kids couldn't be less interested. "How do they support themselves?"

"Bones is probably a part-time brain surgeon," Coke said. "Sweeping the floor and cleaning up kids' puke is his hobby."

"Funny," his sister commented.

"Actually, I think he might be retarded," said Coke.

"You're not supposed to say *retarded*," Pep told her brother. "You're supposed to say *mentally challenged*."

"Whatever."

Coke went back to *The Catcher in the Rye*. He didn't feel like debating the point.

"Do you think Bones could have been one of those guys who tried to kill us yesterday?" Pep asked.

Coke looked up from his book and thought for a moment. His brain was stuffed with so much data, he had nearly forgotten that twenty-four hours earlier he and his sister had jumped off a cliff after being chased by lunatics in golf carts wearing bowler hats and armed with blowguns. A photographic memory only goes so far.

"That's ridiculous," Coke said, looking back down at his book. "Janitors don't kill people."

"Do you smell smoke?" Pep suddenly asked.

"No," Coke replied, clearly annoyed with his sister. "Don't you have a book or something to read?"

"I smell something," Pep insisted.

"You're having an olfactory hallucination."

"Women have a stronger sense of smell than men do, y'know," Pep told him.

Coke knew it was true. In third grade, he'd done a science project in which he had males and females sniff various substances to determine which gender was more sensitive to smell. The girls won easily. The project was written up in the local paper and even mentioned in a national science magazine.

"So maybe the school will burn down, and we can get out of here," Coke remarked.

"You shouldn't even joke about things like that."

A few minutes passed, and Coke suddenly looked up from his book.

"Something's burning!" he said, alarmed.

"I *told* you I smelled smoke!" Pep replied.

They jumped up and saw puffs of smoke coming out of the vent in the back of the room.

"We gotta get outta here!" Coke said.

"Where's Mrs. Higgins?" Pep asked.

"Who cares about her?" Coke said with a snort. "Let's worry about *us*."

"She's the only one who can open the door for us!"

said Pep. She ran to the door and turned the knob. The door was locked. Coke tried to yank it open. Nothing. The door was made of thick wood. It felt warm to the touch. Smoke could be seen through the narrow slit of a window.

"The dead bolt is locked from the other side!" Coke said.

Smoke was pouring out of the vent now. It was starting to fill the room. The roaring sound of a fire could be heard, too.

"Help!" Pep hollered. "Mrs. Higgins! We're locked up in here!"

"She probably ran out of the building to save herself," Coke said. "She doesn't care about us. She hates kids."

Pep was getting frantic. She let out a scream in a frequency that only girls can produce—another advantage females have over males.

"Stop that!" Coke yelled, putting his hands over his ears.

"We're gonna suffocate in here!" Pep yelled at him. "I'm gonna call Mom and Dad on the cell!"

"You can't get a good signal in this room," Coke told her. "I've tried plenty of times. I'm gonna break down the door. It's the only way out."

Pep rolled her eyes as Coke paced off ten steps and

prepared to take a running leap at the door.

"If you do your famous Inflictor move, you're gonna break your leg again," she said as she stepped aside to give him some running room.

"I'm not gonna *kick* it down," Coke told her. "I'm gonna use my shoulder."

He backed up as far as he could go and sprinted for the door. At the last instant, he turned and leaped against the door. Then he crumpled to the floor.

"Did you dislocate your shoulder?" Pep asked, running to him.

"Shut up."

Smoke was snaking under the door. The fire was in the hall. In the detention room, it was becoming hard to see. Worse, it was getting hard to breathe.

Coke was becoming enraged. Despite his sore shoulder, he got up and picked up a desk with both hands. Then he heaved it against the door. It clattered to the ground harmlessly after doing no more damage than nicking off a little paint.

Pep looked around frantically for something she could use to open the door.

"The fire extinguisher!" she yelled as she ran across the room and lifted it off a hook on the wall.

"We'll die from smoke inhalation before the flames get to us!" Coke yelled at her. "The whole school could

be burning down! You think you're gonna put out the fire with a little fire extinguisher?"

"No!" she replied. "We can use it as a battering ram!"

Coke immediately understood what his sister had in mind as she held the fire extinguisher against the wooden door.

Newton's first law of motion states that every object in a state of uniform motion tends to remain in that state of motion unless an external force is applied to it. If they could put enough force against a single point on that door, they might be able to crash right through it. Coke picked up the desk again.

Despite everything that was happening, he couldn't help but think how much fun it was to bust up stuff. Busting up stuff was one of the most fun things you could do. *Building* things is a long, slow, and difficult process. But busting up stuff was nothing but fun, as long as you didn't have to clean up the mess afterward. He had often thought that the ideal career choice would be to work in the demolition business, blowing up old buildings and stadiums. The money probably wasn't very good, but nothing beat the thrill of demolishing things.

Pep held the fire extinguisher against the door. Coke gave himself some running room and gripped the legs of the desk tightly.

"You ready?" he asked. "On three."

"One . . . two . . . three!" they both hollered.

Coke took a deep breath and made a run for the door holding the desk in front him like a battering ram. Pep closed her eyes and tensed her muscles to absorb the impact. When the top surface of the desk crashed against the fire extinguisher, it hit a seam in the wood and broke through, cracking the door in half and sending two preteenagers, a school desk, a fire extinguisher, and pieces of splintered wood into the hallway.

But the hallway was engulfed in flames.

Chapter 7

THE SCIENCE OF FIRE

Fire is an interesting thing. If you've ever passed your finger through a candle flame quickly, you know it doesn't hurt. But leave that finger in the flame for one short second, and it's a different story.

Did you ever look deeply into a flame? The white part is hotter than the yellow part, and the yellow part is hotter than the red part. But the hottest part of a flame is the blue part. That's odd, because we think of blue as the color of cold and red as the color of heat.

You need three things to create fire: oxygen, heat, and fuel. Combine them, and you get ignition. Take any one of them away, and the fire goes out. The science of fire is pretty simple, really.

When the average kid comes crashing through a locked door and lands face-first in a hallway filled with smoke and flames, he probably isn't going to spend a whole lot of time thinking about the science of fire. But Coke McDonald was not an average kid.

"Avoid the blue flames!" Coke shouted as he landed on top of his sister, who, in turn, had landed on top of the shattered door.

"Get off of me!" Pep shouted right back.

The twins jumped off the hot floor and were faced with a nightmare scenario. There were flames and thick smoke in all directions. The sprinkler system in the hallway ceiling had turned on, but the spray of water was no match for the inferno raging around them. Coke and Pep grabbed hold of each other instinctively. There was nothing else to hold on to that wasn't on fire.

A lot of paper—toilet paper, paper towels, art supplies, napkins—was stored in the basement of the old school on the shelves next to the detention room. It had ignited fast. Tiny pieces of charred paper were swirling in the air around the frantic twins. But that wasn't all that was burning. There was a noxious,

flammable substance that had been poured all over the floor.

This fire had been set deliberately.

Who would want to burn down a school?

Don't answer that question.

The sound of fire engines could be heard in the distance, but that didn't provide Coke or Pep with any comfort now. The heat was intense. Their eyes were tearing from the smoke, their throats choking to breathe. There was a nasty chemical smell filling the hall. That stuff alone could probably kill you if you inhaled enough of it.

Pep tried to remember the lessons she'd learned when a firefighter came and spoke at the school a few years earlier. She recalled that he said something about "stop, drop, and roll," but that wouldn't help now. The *floor* was on fire. She wasn't about to roll around on it.

Coke's photographic memory had on file just about everything he'd ever experienced, but he had never bothered to notice where the basement fire exits were located. Even if he knew where they were, those doors could very possibly be locked, or intentionally blocked.

Coke pulled his T-shirt off over his head.

"What, are you trying to be macho?" Pep yelled.

"No, I'm trying to *live*!" he replied.

He ripped the shirt in half, wrapping one piece around his mouth and nose and handing the other piece to his sister. She made a mask of her own. As Coke looked up to see if the ceiling was about to collapse on him, he realized that the bottom of his left pants leg was on fire. He used his other foot to snuff it out, kicking himself and hurting his ankle in the process.

"Oww!" he yelled.

"I think I smell carbon monoxide," Pep shouted in his ear.

"Carbon monoxide is odorless, Einstein!" was his reply. "Let's get out of here!"

"Which way?" she hollered. "I can't see!"

"Doesn't matter!" he shouted back. "You pick. You're the one who has feelings. Use 'em!"

"It's too hot!" she shouted.

Some burning debris fell off a shelf and almost hit her.

"We can't stay here!" Coke told Pep. "We'll be burned alive! One way or another, we've gotta make a run for it!"

"Right through the flames?" she asked.

"Yeah," he replied, "like you're running your finger over a candle. If we move fast enough, we won't feel a thing."

"That's crazy!" she said, and he knew she was right. But staying where they were would be crazy too.

"Where's the fire extinguisher?" Coke yelled. "Maybe we can clear a path with it."

They fumbled around on the floor until Pep got her hands on the fire extinguisher.

"Oww!" she screamed. "It's too hot to touch!"

Coke picked up a piece of the door they had broken and slapped at the flames with it. This worked to an extent, but the wood was heavy and quickly sapped his strength.

"We're gonna die in here!" Pep screamed.

That's when everything went dark.

A large cloth had landed on top of them, and they couldn't see a thing. Then they felt hands pulling the edges of the cloth around them. It was damp.

They felt themselves being lifted and carried somewhere by somebody. They couldn't get their arms free to struggle. They didn't *want* to struggle. They wanted to get out of the hallway, and that was what was happening. Somebody had hoisted them up and was carrying them away.

The twins felt themselves being pushed through a set of double doors and then outside onto the grass in the playground behind the school. The blanket was pulled off so they could see their rescuer.

It was Mr. Rochford, the school janitor. Bones!

"I don't mean to be a wet blanket," he told them, "but I thought you kids could use one."

Coke turned around to see the school enveloped in flames and firefighters in the distance spraying water on it.

"You speak . . . English?" Pep asked Bones.

"Of course," he replied.

"We thought you were . . . retarded or something," Coke explained.

"I believe the politically correct term is mentally challenged," Bones said. "Listen, you kids need to get out of town right away. Somebody is trying to kill you!"

"Yeah, I think we kinda figured that out," Coke said.

"Shouldn't we try to save Mrs. Higgins?" Pep asked. "She might still be in the building somewhere."

"That wouldn't be a smart idea," Bones told them.

"Why?"

"Because I think it might have been Mrs. Higgins who set the fire."

Chapter 8

IN OR OUT

A s soon as they were safely away from the burning school, Bones pulled the twins out of sight, into the woods behind the playground. He tugged at his big bushy beard, and it came off in his hand. He pulled off his mustache. Then he reached under his shirt and tore away a thick piece of foam that had been wrapped around his stomach to make him look like an extremely fat man.

Bones was actually skinny!

"Guess I won't be needing *this* stuff anymore," he said, tossing his disguise aside.

Underneath it all, Bones looked pretty much like a regular guy. It was an amazing transformation.

"You mean to say you've been wearing a fat suit and pretending to be a mute the whole school year?" Pep asked him. "Why?"

"Because I knew this day would finally come," Bones said. "It's a long story."

The fire department did its best to get the blaze under control, but it was hopeless. By the time the fire was completely extinguished, there wasn't much left to save. It didn't look like there was going to be school come September. Not at West Marin Middle School, anyway.

The police were relieved to find that there were no bodies in the rubble. No students or teachers had been in the building when the fire started. At least that's what they told the news media. The detectives had no idea that the McDonald twins had been trapped inside the whole time. Mrs. Higgins, the health teacher, was long gone.

Coke and Pep McDonald had a lot of questions for Bones, the first one pretty obvious: "Why would our health teacher try to kill us?"

Bones was evasive. He told the twins he had been keeping an eye on Mrs. Higgins ever since they'd both been hired back in September. He suspected that she was up to something, but he didn't know what she was going to do or when she was going to do it.

"Are you going to arrest her?" Pep asked.

"She's probably just a paid assassin," replied Bones. "I want to find out who's doing the paying. And besides, I'm not a cop. I can't arrest anybody."

"Then who *are* you?" Coke demanded. "What's going on? Why is all of this happening to us? We have the right to know. We didn't do anything wrong."

"Yeah," agreed Pep. "That's the second time somebody tried to kill us in two days. And it wasn't Mrs. Higgins the first time. The first time it was some dudes wearing black suits and bowler hats."

"Come with me," Bones told the twins. "I'll tell you as much as I'm allowed."

They walked around the corner to Bones's car, an old Ford with a nice variety of dents on the front and back fenders. The guy was either a lousy driver or . . . no, he was just a lousy driver. With some reluctance, Coke and Pep got into the backseat. Individually, neither one of them would have set foot inside that car. Together, they felt safer. If Bones tried anything funny, at least they had him outnumbered.

Bones drove about a mile to a strip mall the twins had been to many times because their favorite Chinese restaurant was there. He pulled the car around to the back where there were some Dumpsters and wooden pallets leaning against the wall.

Bones stopped at an unmarked garage door and got out of the car.

"What is this, your supersecret spy headquarters?" Coke asked.

"You might say that," he replied.

Pep took Coke's hand so they couldn't be separated. Bones wasn't a complete stranger, but all the same she felt uneasy following him around. For all she knew, maybe it was *Bones* who was actually trying to kill them. Maybe this was all an elaborate trap, and they were walking right into it.

Coke had no such concerns.

"Do you have cool doors that slide open and go *whoosh*, like in spy movies?" he asked.

"Not exactly," Bones replied.

He reached down and yanked on the old garage door until it opened with a wrenching squeak.

"You oughta oil that thing," Coke said as he walked inside the garage and looked around.

"Hurry!" Bones urged Pep. "Whoever is trying to kill you may be following us. They may try to burn down the place, just like they burned down the school."

"All right," Pep demanded. "What's going on? We want some answers."

"Okay. Do the letters *T G F* mean anything to you?" Bones asked after Pep had stepped inside. He pulled

down the door behind her.

"No clue."

"*T G F*!" Coke exclaimed. "Yeah! That was the last thing that lady Mya said to us before we jumped off the cliff!"

"That's right!" Pep said. "And then she got hit by a dart and collapsed."

"*T G F* stands for The Genius Files," Bones began. "It's a top secret government program. I work for TGF. Mya is one of us. Or *was*, I should say, before they got to her. Mrs. Higgins used to be with TGF too. Now, it appears, she has a different agenda. She must be working for somebody else."

Bones told the McDonald twins all about Dr. Herman Warsaw and what had happened to him on 9/11. How he'd stepped outside for a cigarette; and as the plane crashed into the Pentagon, he'd come up with the idea of enlisting the smartest kids in the country to solve the world's problems. But somewhere along the way, that genius plan seemed to have gone off the tracks.

"And you two are a part of TGF too," Bones explained.

Ordinarily, Coke would have let out a snort and said, "You gotta be kidding me." In his almost thirteen years, nothing particularly amazing had ever happened to him or his sister. They led completely normal lives filled with video games, pizza, TV, and all the normal things that kids in the suburbs are used to. The idea that they were actually part of a vast government program was inconceivable. But there had been two attempts on their lives now, and it was starting to sink into Coke's brain that he and his sister were in the middle of something big. Their days as normal kids were over.

"Why were *we* chosen for TGF?" Pep asked. "We're not that smart."

"Speak for yourself," Coke told her.

"You are *extremely* smart," Bones told her. "But I will tell you that when Dr. Warsaw started the program, he wanted to have a few children who could work as a team, and enlisting twins seemed to be a good way to accomplish that. He may have lowered his baseline score a few points in order to include both of you."

"But why would Mrs. Higgins try to kill us?" Pep asked.

"That's what I'm trying to find out," Bones replied. "Maybe she had a falling out with Dr. Warsaw, and she's trying to get back at him."

"Our parents are going to go *ballistic* when they find out about all this," Pep said, shaking her head.

"No they won't," Bones said, his voice lowering slightly. "You can't tell them. *Ever.*"

Bones explained to the twins that it was Dr. Warsaw's belief, logically enough, that parents would never allow their children to be part of such a dangerous program. It was also Dr. Warsaw's belief that The Genius Files was so crucial to the security of the United States that parents of the young geniuses must never be informed. The children had to be sworn to secrecy, with the implied threat to their loved ones if word ever got out. And they were strictly forbidden to notify the police or other authority figures about any TGF activities.

"Wait a minute," Pep said. "We never agreed to be part of this Genius Files thing. You can't force us."

"You're already in it," Bones replied simply. "It was all about standardized test scores. Your names are in the computer. Didn't your parents receive a letter saying you would be in a special gifted and talented program? It went out months ago."

"They probably threw it away," Coke said. "Our parents are kind of spacey."

"If the letter went out months ago, why did you wait until now to contact us?" Pep asked.

"I wanted to wait until we had a mission for you,"

Bones told her. "Now, of course, you have a temporary mission: to stay alive."

"Let me get this straight," Coke said. "It doesn't matter if we agreed to be part of this Genius Files thing or not. Either way, Mrs. Higgins and those bowler dudes are trying to kill us."

"That's unfortunate, and true," Bones said. "I'm sorry you were put in this position. It was out of my control. But I hope you *will* agree to help us."

"What do we have to do?" Pep asked.

"I can't tell you right now, for security reasons," Bones replied. "Some things are better off not being known. You'll be contacted in due time."

"That's *it*?" Coke said with some anger in his voice. "That's all you're gonna tell us? And you expect us to help with your screwball program? This is bogus. What's in it for us?"

"A million dollars when you turn twenty-one. . . ."

"A million dollars?" Pep asked.

"Each," added Bones. "Tax free. Not to mention excitement, travel . . ."

"Travel?" Coke said. "Oh, great. So people will be trying to kill us all over the world? We'll never live to be twenty-one."

". . . and protection," Bones added. "I might mention that we already saved your lives twice."

"That's only because you put us in the position of our lives being threatened!" Coke said. "You almost got us *killed* twice!"

"I'm sorry about that."

"Okay, so when do we get to meet this famous Dr. Warsaw?" Pep asked.

"Probably never," Bones told her. "I've only met him once myself: the day he hired me. He's a brilliant man, and also a recluse. I hear he lives on a boat somewhere."

"Great," Coke muttered.

"Are there others out there?" Pep asked. "Other TGF kids like us?"

"Yes," Bones said. "Lots of others. Maybe you'll get to meet them."

"I don't want to meet them," Pep said. "I just want things to go back to normal."

"You can forget about that," Coke grumbled.

"Look," Bones told the twins, "sometimes people do things for money, or fame, or because their parents tell them to. Other times they do things to look cool or for some superficial, cosmetic reason. And sometimes people want to do something for the good of their country or the good of the world. People have all kinds of motivations for doing what they do. Whatever you decide, I'll respect your decision. No hard feelings either way. If you decide not to help us, you'll never hear from me again. I'm not saying Mrs. Higgins and those men in bowler hats who have been after you are going to stop, but I promise you won't hear from me again. Of course, if you're in trouble and need help, you won't hear from me either."

"How long do we have to decide?" Coke asked.

"Five minutes."

The twins went off to the corner of the garage to talk things over. The easy solution, they agreed, would be to walk away. Just say no. Common sense said to pretend the whole thing never happened. Go back to their normal lives.

But both of them realized that there was no normal life anymore to be had. Somebody was out to get them, and not just their crazy health teacher, Mrs. Higgins. For all they knew, they would step out of the garage to find a group of assassins aiming machine guns at them. It's not like these people were going to leave them alone just because they said they weren't playing the game anymore.

And, of course, a million dollars was a million dollars.

Being the younger of the two (by three minutes), Pep would generally defer to her brother when it

came to tough decisions. She said she was torn and would leave the final decision up to him.

Coke had a crazy, delusional thought running through his head. There was one thing he didn't get a lot of in his ordinary suburban life. There was one thing that *every* kid wants more of. It wasn't money, or straight As, or a cool ringtone. It was attention.

"When this thing is over," he said to himself, "we might be on every talk show and every magazine cover. There will be fan clubs and websites devoted to us. The girls will be crazy for me. I'll be signing autographs for my adoring fans. When this is all over, I'll be so famous that I might have to wear a disguise in public so people won't mob me. I'll be like a rock star."

That is, if he was still alive. It would be a gamble.

After five minutes, Bones asked for an answer using a one-word question.

"So?"

Coke took a deep breath.

"We're in," he replied.

Chapter 9
WELCOME TO THE FAMILY

"Congratulations," Bones said as he shook hands with each twin enthusiastically. "Welcome to the GF family."

Pep wrinkled her nose. She had enough problems with her own family. She didn't need another one, and she wasn't at all sure she wanted to be part of *this* one.

Bones pulled aside a large piece of cardboard on the floor of the garage. There was a wooden door underneath. He yanked it open, revealing stairs that went down. Bones climbed into the hole and beckoned the twins to follow.

"So this is where you keep the *real* spy stuff, eh?"

Coke said, looking around. There were cameras, tools, and all kinds of equipment lining the shelves of the walls in the cramped room.

"You might say that."

Coke picked up two staple guns.

"What do these shoot," he asked, "laser beams?"

"Put those down!" Bones said sternly.

"They shoot *staples*, you idiot!" Pep told her brother.

"Okay, okay, relax."

"We have a very short, uh . . . initiation ceremony that all new recruits have to go through," Bones told them. "I hope you don't mind. It's no big deal."

"It doesn't involve jumping off a cliff or setting our school on fire, does it?" Pep asked nervously.

"No, no! Nothing like that," said Bones. "All you have to do is turn around to face the wall and make the sound of the letter *Z* with your throats."

"*Zzzzzzzzzzzzzzzzzzzzzzzzzz*," the twins said.

While they were making the sound, Bones picked up the two staple guns Coke had been fooling with. He placed them gently against the back of the children's heads and pulled the triggers.

"*Owwwwwwwwwwwwwww! Are you crazy?*" Coke said after spinning around to see Bones holding both staple guns. "What is your problem, man?"

"You stapled my *head*!" Pep shouted. "I can't believe

you would do that!"

"I did not staple your head," Bones explained calmly. "I implanted tiny GPS devices in your scalps. They're harmless. Now we can track you more easily."

"Why do you need to track us?" Pep asked.

"It's for your safety," Bones explained. "If you're in trouble anywhere in the world, we'll be able to find you. This GPS is accurate within three feet. Dr. Warsaw designed it personally. Someday everyone will have one."

"Great," Coke said glumly, rubbing the back of his head.

"Isn't that an invasion of privacy?" Pep asked.

"Strictly speaking, I suppose it is," Bones admitted. "But we feel the advantages outweigh the disadvantages."

"Hey, why did you tell us to make the *Z* sound?" Coke asked.

"So you wouldn't notice the staple guns," Bones said. "Listen, before I send you home, I want to give you something. A small token of our appreciation."

"You already implanted a small token of your appreciation in each of our heads," Pep said.

Bones went over to a shelf and came back with a shopping bag.

"What is it?" Coke asked. "Some kind of a gun that's

hidden inside a candy bar or something?"

"Goodness no," Bones said. "We can't be handing out guns to children, now can we?"

He pulled a Frisbee out of the bag. It said TGF FLYING HIGH on it.

"You're giving us a Frisbee?" Pep asked, puzzled.

"We had some left over from the company picnic," Bones explained.

"You have company picnics!?" Pep asked. "I thought this was a top secret organization?"

"It was a top secret picnic," said Bones.

"It's not a Frisbee, you dope!" said Coke. "That lady Mya had one of these up on the cliff. Remember? It's a Frisbee *grenade*! We can throw this sucker at bad guys and totally waste them."

"Mya's Frisbee grenade was a prototype," Bones told them. "They cost fifty thousand dollars each. We could never afford to hand them out casually. Budget cuts, you know. And they're very dangerous, too. You haven't been trained to use them."

"Then I'll bet the Frisbee shoots lasers, huh?" Coke said. "Like, you throw it and it zaps everything within fifty feet. That is cool! Where's the on-off switch?"

"It doesn't shoot lasers," Bones said. "It doesn't turn on or off."

"Then it must give off a magnetic force field or

something, right?" Coke asked. "Or when you throw it, it sprays some vile stuff like a skunk does."

"It doesn't give off a force field," Bones said. "It doesn't spray anything. You just fling it."

"I get it," Coke guessed. "After you chuck it, razor blades pop out of the sides. When it reaches the victim, it can slice a man's head off like a knife going through a hunk of cheese. That is *awesome*!"

"No, no! It's nothing like that," Bones told Coke. "It's a *toy*. You throw it to somebody and they catch it. Then they throw it back to you. Something fun for you to play with in your travels. The only thing you can kill with it is time."

"No razor blades?" Coke said, disappointed. "No laser beams or force fields?"

"Just plastic," Bones said.

"Plastic explosives?" Coke asked hopefully. "I heard about them. They're invisible to metal detectors."

"No. Just plain old *plastic* plastic."

Coke looked at the Frisbee.

"Well, this thing is lame," he decided.

"You're giving us a *Frisbee*?" Pep said. "We're expected to go out and protect the free world

with a *Frisbee*? I don't even know how to throw a Frisbee."

"It's just for fun!" Bones told the twins. "You're kids! Don't you want to have fun? Here, I have a deck of cards for you, too."

"A deck of cards?" Pep said. "What am I supposed to do with *that*?"

"I know," Coke said. "The playing cards contain the secret codes to launch a nuclear attack, right?"

"Uh, no," Bones said.

"I think they're just plain old playing cards," Pep told her brother, disappointed.

"What, is each card actually a video camera?" Coke asked. "That is ingenious! How do you fit the camera into such a thin piece of cardboard?"

"We don't. It's just a—"

"Don't tell me," Coke said, holding up his hand. "The edges of the cards are coated with poison. When you flip them at somebody, they get a paper cut, the poison enters their bloodstream, and they die within thirty seconds. Am I right?"

"No."

"Sixty seconds?"

"Look, you've got to understand," Bones said. "The Genius Files project doesn't have a lot of money. These are just going-away presents I'm giving you. It's like a goody bag you get when you go to somebody's birthday party."

"Don't we get any *real* weapons to use so we can defend ourselves?" Coke asked.

"No. Here, take some fruit too."

"Thank you," Pep said graciously. "This is all very generous of you."

"Are there bombs inside the fruit?" Coke asked.

"No. You *eat* it," Bones said wearily. "Now listen, because this is very important. You will *not* tell your parents *anything* I have told you. You will not tell your friends. You are undercover. There appear to be some extremely dangerous people out there who want The Genius Files to fail. Do you understand?"

"I understand," Pep said.

"When are we going to see you again?" Coke asked.

"Soon, hopefully. Or maybe never."

"Gee, can you be more vague?" asked Coke.

"Would you like a ride home?" Bones asked.

"It's a short walk," Pep said.

The twins took their goody bag and climbed back up the ladder into the garage. Bones yanked open the creaky door and let them out.

"Good-bye," Bones said. "And good luck."

The twins left the garage and had walked about ten yards when Pep stopped.

"What did we just get ourselves into?" she asked her brother.

"Relax," Coke replied. "I have a feeling this is gonna be cool. We're gonna be like spies. Hey, I thought of a new name for myself. From now on, I want you to call me Ace Fist."

"What?!"

"Ace Fist," Coke repeated. "That would be a cool nickname. Doesn't it sound like an action hero? Ace Fist, secret agent."

"It sounds stupid," Pep told her brother. "That's what it sounds like."

"You're just jealous because you didn't think of it."

"I am not."

"Are, too."

The twins were jawing back and forth when a flash of light came from the garage they had just left. As they turned to look, a huge orange fireball rocked them backward as the entire building exploded in a shower of bricks, dirt, glass, wood, and concrete. Coke and Pep dove to their left into a ditch at the side of the parking lot.

When things explode in the movies, it's usually shown in slow motion. You see debris gracefully floating through the air. It takes about ten seconds for everything to hit the ground.

In real time, it's a different story. Explosions aren't beautiful. After the initial flash of light, it's pretty much finished. The building is there and then it's gone.

Tiny pieces of the building were flying everywhere like bullets. The whole thing was over before Coke or Pep even realized what had happened.

"Bones!" they screamed.

Chapter 10

MANIFEST DESTINY

Well, now it looked as if the two people who could help the McDonald twins were both dead. Mya, the woman in red who saved their lives up on the cliff, had been shot in the neck with a poisoned dart. And now Bones, blown to pieces.

For a moment, Coke thought about becoming Ace Fist the action hero and running back into the garage to save Bones. But the building had been *obliterated*. Nothing was left. There was no way anybody could have survived the blast. And it would be risky to try. Whoever set off that explosion was, in all probability, trying to kill him and his sister. The smart thing to do would be to get out of there as quickly as possible.

"Do you think it's *our* fault that Mya and Bones are dead?" Pep asked as they ran home. "Maybe we're bad luck."

"Of *course* it's not our fault," Coke told her. "It's *their* fault. They're the ones who put us in danger. The people who have been trying to kill us just got *them* instead. No wonder Dr. Warsaw decided that it's up to kids to save the world. Grown-ups have no idea what to do."

On the inside, though, both twins felt a twinge of guilt. Mya and Bones had been trying to help them, and now they were gone. Coke and Pep were on their own.

There was a chill in the air as they got closer to home. Coke wished he hadn't so gallantly ripped his T-shirt in half when they were trapped in the burning school. He felt cold now.

"Do you think Mom and Dad know what happened at school?" Pep asked her brother.

"Are you kidding?" he replied. "Aliens could land on our front lawn, and Mom and Dad wouldn't notice. I bet all the parents were called. Mom and Dad probably didn't pick up the phone or check their email."

In fact, Dr. McDonald *had* checked his email. An emergency message had gone out to parents telling them the school had burned down after everyone had

left for summer vacation. Dr. McDonald assumed it was another one of those internet hoaxes he received all the time. He deleted it from his in-box with a laugh.

When the twins finally got home, their parents barely noticed them. They were in the middle of a heated discussion on the front lawn.

"I can't believe this, Bridge!" Dr. McDonald complained. "The garbagemen took my garbage can!"

"That's what they're *supposed* to do, Ben," Mrs. McDonald informed him.

"No, they took my *good* garbage can," he added. "The small one in my office."

"Well, why did you put your good garbage can out with the trash?" Mrs. McDonald asked logically.

"I wanted them to take the garbage *in* the can, not the can itself," he explained. "The can wasn't garbage. The *stuff* in the can was garbage. It was *obvious*!"

"You shouldn't have put your good garbage can out on the lawn, Ben," she said. "It's your own fault."

"Well, they shouldn't have taken it away!"

The twins looked from one parent to the other as if they were watching a Ping-Pong tournament.

"How are the garbagemen supposed to know what is or isn't garbage?" Mrs. McDonald continued. "They're not mind readers."

"What do I have to do, spell it out for them?"

"Apparently so," she replied. "Why don't you make a sign that says NOT GARBAGE and put it on the can you don't want to throw away?"

"I'm not making a sign for the garbagemen!" he said, exasperated. "You know, last year I was *trying* to throw away an old beat-up garbage can, but they wouldn't take it. They didn't think it was garbage. And now they took my *good* garbage can that I didn't want to throw away. I'm telling you, Bridge, you can't win with these people!"

Coke and Pep silently prayed that they would never become grown-ups.

Their parents turned and faced them, finally realizing there were more important things in life than garbage cans.

"It's about time you kids got home," Dr. McDonald said, pulling his children to him in a bear hug.

"What happened to your shirt?" Mrs. McDonald asked Coke.

"It ripped," Coke replied. It was, technically, the truth. "I had to throw it away."

"Is that any way to treat your clothes? Shirts don't grow on trees, you know," his mother said. "They cost money. You need to take better care of your possessions. Ben, should there be consequences to this?"

Dr. McDonald didn't like to hear his children being

scolded. He always believed you get better results by rewarding good behavior than you do by punishing bad behavior.

"Anything exciting happen at school today?" he asked to change the subject.

"Nope, other than the fact that it burned down," Coke said.

"Ha-ha-ha-ha-ha!" Dr. McDonald chortled. "I got that email too. You kids crack me up. Bridge, I'm so glad we decided to have children after all."

Pep and her mom went inside to prepare dinner, while Dr. McDonald brought Coke around to the side of the RV, which was parked in the driveway.

"We're heading out first thing in the morning," he told Coke. "And I have a job for you. I need you to clean the toilet."

"Why do *I* have to clean the toilet?" Coke complained. "Why can't Pep do it?"

"Because you're a guy," Dr. McDonald said, "and we guys are disgusting, filthy creatures, right? Besides, which would you rather do: clean the toilet or help Mom cook dinner?"

"I'd rather watch TV," Coke replied.

"That wasn't one of the options," his dad said. "Come on! This is going to be fun! C'mere, I'll show you how to do a dump."

Instead of using water to flush, the toilets in RVs use gravity. There's a holding tank underneath the bowl. When you get to a dump station at a campground, you attach a thick hose to the RV and let the contents of the holding tank fall into a ground inlet that leads to the sewer system. It's fairly disgusting when you think about it.

So don't think about it.

Dr. McDonald gave Coke a pair of yellow rubber gloves and showed him how to attach the hose to the connectors below the toilet.

"You want a real tight fit," he told his son, "or you're in for a big surprise."

Dr. McDonald showed Coke which lever he needed to pull to open the valve and which one to pull to flush some water through the system when he was done.

"And that's how you do a dump," Dr. McDonald said, packing up the hose again. "Easy as pie."

"It's gross, Dad," Coke said. "We're going to be essentially driving a Porta-Potty cross-country."

"It's completely sanitary and environmentally friendly," Dr. McDonald told him. "And it's fun, too! Think about it: a full week's worth of waste from the four of us can fit in this tank."

"Nice image, Dad," Coke remarked.

"Someday they'll figure out a way to turn human waste into fuel," Dr. McDonald said, "and we won't need gasoline anymore. We'll drive cars powered by our own poop. Can you imagine? The holding tank will also be the gas tank."

"And when that glorious day comes," Coke said, "our dependence on foreign oil will be . . . eliminated!"

"Very funny," Dr. McDonald noted.

When dinner was ready, Coke and his dad washed their hands and charged into the kitchen. They knew this would be their last home-cooked meal for some time. The RV had a little kitchen in it, but meals on the road were likely to be a lot of fast food and burgers over a campfire. But tonight it was roast chicken, mashed potatoes, and corn on the cob.

There was a large map of the United States taped up on one wall of the kitchen. Mrs. McDonald had drawn a line with a marker starting in San Francisco and extending all the way across the country.

"Remember, Aunt Judy is getting married near the Lincoln Memorial on July Fourth," she explained as she spooned potatoes onto everyone's plate. "So we have to get to Washington by that date. But we'll be stopping off at lots of fascinating spots along the way."

Dr. McDonald rolled his eyes. He knew what kinds of fascinating spots his wife had in mind. Not important historical spots such as the Liberty Bell. Not the Grand Canyon. Not Yosemite National Park.

No, Mrs. McDonald's idea of fascinating would be a town that had a museum devoted to *Star Trek*. A giant statue of Paul Bunyan. The largest ball of twine in the world.

"We've never been to the East Coast," Pep said. "We've never been to the Midwest. You never take us *anywhere*."

"We took you to Disneyland," Mrs. McDonald pointed out.

Dr. McDonald had been waiting almost thirteen years to go on a cross-country trip with the family. It would have been pointless when the twins were little, because they wouldn't have remembered anything they had seen. Now that they were less than a week away from becoming full-fledged teenagers, they could appreciate it. They would remember this trip for the rest of their lives.

"Do you kids know what 'Manifest Destiny' means?" Dr. McDonald asked as he munched across an ear of corn like he was typing on an old-fashioned typewriter.

"Yeah," Coke said, recalling a library book he'd read years earlier. He could see the page in his head. "When the country was young, Manifest Destiny was a belief that the United States should expand across North America all the way from the Atlantic to the Pacific Ocean."

Sometimes that photographic memory came in handy.

"That's right, son," Dr. McDonald said, beaming. Having really smart kids did have its advantages. "You might say it's part of the American Dream. Tomorrow we're going to begin a *reverse* Manifest Destiny. We'll start near the Pacific Ocean and drive all the way to the Atlantic. Go east, young man!"

"But wasn't Manifest Destiny just an excuse to steal the land and kill the Indians who were living in North America long before we did?" asked Pep. "Wasn't it almost like genocide?"

"Pass the chicken," Dr. McDonald said. Having really smart kids did have its disadvantages.

After dinner, the kids packed their duffel bags for the trip. They needed to bring a lot of clothes because their mother said she didn't want to stop every few days to do laundry.

It had been a long day, and the next one would be longer. Pep usually read before going to sleep; but on this particular night she spent an hour Facebooking, emailing, and texting good-bye to her closest friends. There were about a hundred of them. She wished she could tell them all about The Genius Files, but of course she had promised Bones she would keep quiet. It wasn't easy. After jumping off a cliff to avoid some crazy guys with poisoned darts and watching a building explode, what are you supposed to type when Twitter asks, "What's happening?"

Coke thought about calling his friend Jimmy Erdman but decided to text instead. . . .

COKE: See U in Sept. If Im lucky.
JIMMY: What U mean, if Im lucky?
COKE: Cant tell U. Maybe when it's all over.

Most kids want to have their own bedroom. But Coke and Pep had been together since the day they were born; and despite their differences and disagreements, neither one minded sharing a room with the other. They had bunk beds: Coke on the bottom, and Pep on the top.

"You okay?" Coke asked a few seconds after he turned off the light.

"Yeah," his sister replied in the darkness. "I think it's gonna be all for the better."

"How do you figure that?"

"Well, once we're away from home, out in the middle of nowhere with Mom and Dad," she explained, "Mrs. Higgins and those bowler dudes won't be bothering us anymore."

"Yeah, I'll bet this whole thing is gonna blow over," Coke said. "The school will be rebuilt over the summer, and everything will be back to normal."

There was no more talking after that. Pep dropped off to sleep. Coke tossed and turned, unable to get comfortable in his bed. His leg was aching from when he kicked himself trying to put out the flames on his pants when they were trapped in the school. That reminded him of all they had been through in the last twenty-four hours, which made it even harder to fall asleep.

He punched his pillow and flipped it over. That's when he discovered an envelope tucked neatly underneath the pillow. He picked up the flashlight that was always under his bed and tore open the envelope. There was a note inside.

This is what it said:

KCAORE HTANAO EASUO HEAHT
NIAUO AYTEA EMLLIAWI

Chapter 11

ON THE ROAD

"Wake up!" Dr. McDonald shouted from the bottom of the stairs. "Today is the first day of the rest of your lives!"

Coke rolled over for one more minute of precious sleep. In the back of his mind, he vaguely remembered the envelope he'd found under his pillow the night before. He had memorized the message that was inside it: KCAORE HTANAO EASUO HEAHT NIAUO AYTEA EMLLIAWI.

But just because you're classified a genius with a photographic memory doesn't mean you're good at figuring out secret messages and codes. Coke considered himself a numbers guy, an action guy.

Ace Fist. Before he'd fallen asleep, he had slipped the envelope into his backpack so he could show it to his sister in the morning. She would be able to decipher it. She was good at that kind of stuff.

"Who's ready to go coast to coast?" hollered Dr. McDonald as he bounded into the twins' room clapping his hands enthusiastically. "It's our manifest destiny!"

"Not mine," Coke groaned.

His dad opened the shades to let in some light and to try to wake up the kids. Then he went outside and finished packing the RV, carefully going through his checklist to make sure he didn't forget anything essential: extra water, flashlights, jumper cables, road flares, first aid kit, pens and paper, trash bags, camera, and so on. Mrs. McDonald busied herself with food, filling the little RV refrigerator and emptying the one at home. A carton of milk left in a fridge for two months would not be a pretty sight when they got back.

Coke threw his iPod, cell phone charger, and a few books into his backpack. He was ready to go. Pep

was a different story. In the last few months, she had started to care—for the first time—about her personal appearance. Suddenly, she was spending hours straightening her hair in the mirror and agonizing over what she should wear. Coke teased his sister as she smeared a mysterious substance she called "foundation" on her face to cover up a few pimples that nobody would ever notice in a million years. Some days she even put on nail polish or lip gloss.

"You're still ugly," Coke remarked as his sister examined herself. "It's genetic." He liked teasing her about her looks, as they looked almost exactly alike.

"Let's *go*!" Dr. McDonald shouted urgently. "The open road awaits us! We've got to get through California today!"

Pep stuffed her hair-straightening iron into her backpack. As an afterthought, Coke grabbed the Frisbee and deck of cards that Bones had given them. There would be time to kill on the road. Even if his sister couldn't throw a Frisbee, he might meet somebody who could.

Mrs. McDonald had prepared bagels for the kids to eat on the road. She didn't want to wait another half hour for them to eat a proper breakfast at home.

Finally, everyone piled into the RV, grown-ups in the front seats, kids in the back.

"Take a deep breath, everybody," Dr. McDonald said, closing his eyes. "Can you smell it? Can you taste it?"

"Taste what, Dad?" Coke asked.

"Fresh air," his father replied. "If we were taking this trip by plane, we'd be breathing stale, recycled air."

"We'd also be in Washington a few hours from now," Coke said.

"I thought recycling was a good thing, Dad," Pep commented.

"Not recycled *air*," her father replied. "You kids need to get back to nature. It used to be that children would explore, learn, and become part of their world. But now they just snap digital pictures of each other, Facebook their friends, text, and Twitter. You need to slow down, enjoy the moment. You're too impatient to get to the next thing."

"Yeah, can we go now, Dad?" Coke asked. "This is boring."

"You don't know how lucky you are," Dr. McDonald said. "Very few kids get to see this great country the way people used to: on the open road. It's soul lifting. You're going to see what makes America's heart beat. My family took a cross-country trip when I was a kid. Boy, those were some of the best memories of my life."

"What happened?" Pep asked.

"Uh . . . I . . . don't remember, actually," Dr. McDonald admitted. "It was a long time ago."

"It must have made a huge impression on you, Dad," Coke remarked.

"Well, it was a great trip," his father insisted. "I remember that much."

"Can we *go* already?" Mrs. McDonald said impatiently. "The sooner we leave, the sooner we get to Kansas."

"And *why* exactly are we going to Kansas?" Pep asked.

"To see the largest ball of twine in the world!" Mrs. McDonald exclaimed. "Remember?"

"Oh yeah," Coke muttered.

Dr. McDonald rolled his eyes and turned the key. The RV rumbled to life. It didn't sound like a regular car. The whole thing vibrated.

"Front and back doors locked?" he asked Mrs. McDonald, the copilot.

"Check," Mrs. McDonald replied.

"Lights out?"

"Check."

"You called the post office to hold our mail?"

"Check."

"You stopped the newspaper delivery?"

"Check."

"Told the neighbors we would be away until the end of the summer?"

"Check."

"Then we're off!"

Dr. McDonald shifted into reverse and carefully backed the RV out of the driveway, taking one last look at the house before heading down the street.

In the backseats, the twins breathed involuntary sighs of relief. They were safe, at least for a few months. There would be no more lunatics in golf carts and bowler hats shooting poisoned darts at them. No more schools set on fire. No more buildings exploding. They could put all those attempts on their lives behind them. Maybe the whole thing had just been an elaborate hoax. Maybe they were being punked.

"Are we there yet?" Coke asked when they pulled up to the first stop sign. His father turned around to shoot him a look, and Coke added, "Just kidding, Dad!"

Okay, you need to do something before we continue with the story. Get out a road atlas of the United States. You know, one of those big Rand McNally books. Your mom or dad has one. Everybody has one. Go ahead and ask if you can borrow it. We'll wait.

Did you get it? Good.

Open it up to a page that shows the entire country. If you wanted to drive all the way across the United States from the Pacific to the Atlantic, there are several different ways you could go. Route 2 goes north across the top of the country from Seattle all the way to Maine. See it?

Route 20 starts at the Oregon coast and wends its way past Yellowstone National Park, Mount Rushmore, and Niagara Falls, and ends at Boston, Massachusetts.

Another way to go would be to take Route 50, which is called the Loneliest Road. It starts in Oakland, California, and goes through Nevada, Utah, Colorado, Kansas, Missouri, Illinois, Indiana, Ohio, West Virginia, and Virginia, and finally ends in Ocean City, Maryland.

There's also the legendary Route 66, but that only goes as far as Chicago.

Do you see them on the map?

After discussing all these options, Dr. and Mrs. McDonald had chosen I-80, a superhighway that starts near San Francisco and ends in Teaneck, New Jersey. This historic route is almost 3,000 miles from one end to the other (2,899.54, to be exact). It follows part of the path of the Oregon

Trail, the California Trail, and the First Transcontinental Railroad.

As they merged onto Route 1 heading south toward San Francisco, Mrs. McDonald put on one of her classic rock CDs from her youth. Some long-haired band called Steppenwolf was singing "Born to Be Wild." In the backseat, the kids groaned. You don't play "Born to Be Wild" in an RV. It's just not right. This was going to be a *long* drive.

"Hey, you wanna play cards or something?" Coke asked his sister. He pulled out the deck of cards Bones had given them as a going-away present.

"I don't know any card games," Pep replied.

"I'll teach you one," Coke said. "Did you ever hear of a card game called 52 Pickup?"

"No."

"It's the easiest game in the world."

Coke took the entire deck of cards in one hand and squeezed it between his thumb and his first finger until the deck bent into an arch shape. Then he squeezed the deck a little more until the cards went shooting up in the air, one at a time.

There was a wild spray of playing cards all over the back of the RV.

"And that's how you play 52 Pickup!" Coke said, cackling his insane laugh.

"You are *so* obnoxious!" Pep told her brother.

"Hey, knock it off back there!" Mrs. McDonald shouted. "Pick up those cards. This isn't your bedroom. We *all* have to live in here."

Coke scooped up the cards and shuffled them mindlessly. Staring out the window as they crossed the Golden Gate Bridge, he suddenly remembered the envelope he'd found under his pillow the night before. He pulled it out of his backpack and handed it to his sister without explanation.

"Is this another one of your dumb games?" she asked, hesitating before accepting the envelope.

"It was under my pillow when we went to sleep last night," he whispered in her ear so their parents wouldn't hear.

Pep opened the envelope and looked at the message on the slip of paper inside:

KCAORE HTANAO EASUO HEAHT NIAUO AYTEA EMLLIAWI.

"What's that supposed to mean?" she asked.

"Ya got me," Coke replied.

"It's some kind of a cipher," Pep whispered.

"You mean a code?" Coke asked.

"A code disguises words or phrases," Pep explained. "A cipher disguises single letters."

"Where'd you learn that?"

"Everybody knows that."

"I didn't," Coke said.

"Well, you're a dope."

"What are you kids whispering about back there?" Mrs. McDonald asked.

"Nothing," the twins replied together.

"How about we play the license plate game?" Dr. McDonald piped up. "Look! That car that just passed us on the left is from Florida!"

"Not right now, Dad," Pep said. She pulled out her cell phone so she and Coke could text each other without their parents listening in.

```
PEP: Who gave u the envelope?
COKE: Nobody. It was under pillow
PEP: We can figure this out
COKE: U can figure it out
PEP: Some genius u r
```

Pep carefully examined the slip of paper. Just before the explosion at the garage, Bones had told them that someone connected with The Genius Files would be

contacting them. This message could be important.

KCAORE HTANAO EASUO HEAHT NIAUO AYTEA EMLLIAWI

Pep was good at word games. Whenever the family played Boggle or Scrabble, she would beat them all. She could finish most crossword puzzles in minutes.

She searched for a pattern in the letters. Her concentration was so intense that she didn't notice the music in the background, the family conversation, or the miles going by. The RV rolled through the hilly streets of San Francisco and past San Francisco International Airport.

The letters of the message seemed entirely random. She was stumped.

"We're here!" Mrs. McDonald suddenly shouted as the RV rolled to a stop.

"What?" Pep asked, looking up. "We're in Kansas *already*?"

"Where's the world's largest ball of twine?" asked Coke.

"Not Kansas, silly!" Mrs. McDonald said. "We're in Burlingame, California."

Burlingame? The kids knew Burlingame. It's only twenty minutes south of San Francisco.

"What are we doing *here*?" Pep asked. "I thought we were going cross-country."

Then she saw the little sign:

The BURLINGAME MUSEUM of Pez Memorabilia

"Pez?" Pep asked. "Who's Pez?"

"Not who," Mrs. McDonald said. "*What*."

"You really don't know what Pez is?" Coke asked his sister. "Are you from another planet? Pez is that candy you put in a little plastic holder, and when you move the head back, a piece of the candy pops out of the thing's neck."

"That sounds disgusting," Pep said as they climbed out of the RV. "They actually have a museum about that stuff?"

In fact, they do. Mrs. McDonald had heard about the Burlingame Museum of Pez Memorabilia from one of her web readers, who email her tips all the time. She thought it would be the perfect place to feature on *Amazing but True*.

Coke, of course, knew just about everything anybody would ever want to know about Pez. He had read a magazine article about it in the dentist's office and remembered every word of it.

Pez, he told the others, was invented in 1927 by an Austrian businessman named Eduard Haas. He got

the name by abbreviating *pfefferminz*—the German word for *peppermint*.

Mrs. McDonald grabbed her laptop computer and led the rest of the family into the museum. For a real "Pezhead," this must be what heaven is like. The museum had 683 different Pez dispensers, including some vintage ones from the 1950s and the "extremely rare" Pez pineapple wearing sunglasses.

Even Coke learned a thing or two he didn't know. Pez, for instance, was originally sold as a mint to people who were trying to quit smoking.

In one room was the world's largest Pez dispenser. It was almost eight feet tall and looked sort of like a skinny snowman.

"Isn't this cool?" Mrs. McDonald asked, taking a

photo to put on *Amazing but True*.

"Oh yeah, Mom," Pep said. "*Totally.*"

Actually, it *was* pretty cool, but Pep wasn't about to admit it. Things are cool when parents think they *aren't* cool. If parents think something is cool, then, by definition, it can't be. Any kid knows that.

Dr. McDonald looked over the array of Pez memorabilia, shaking his head the whole time. He had spent the last twenty years of his life teaching and writing scholarly articles about American history. He could be visiting Valley Forge. He could be visiting Lexington and Concord. But here he was, staring at the largest Pez dispenser in the world. He sighed. These are the sacrifices grown-ups make for marriage, he figured.

"I don't get it," Dr. McDonald mumbled. "What's the dispenser for? Why can't you just eat the candy without putting it in a dispenser?"

"The dispenser is cool, Dad," Coke informed him. "The candy tastes better when it comes out of Mr. Spock's neck."

The Pez museum also had a section devoted to classic toys such as Tinkertoy, Colorforms, View-Master, and Lincoln Logs. The McDonald family spent a few minutes looking over the watches and T-shirts in the gift shop before piling out the door and back into the RV. Mrs. McDonald bought a Pez dispenser for each of

the twins as a souvenir. A Coke Pez for Coke, and a Pepsi Pez for Pep.

"Ben, you left the keys sitting in the RV with the window open!" Mrs. McDonald complained. "*Anybody could have come along and driven this thing off.*"

"Sorry!" Dr. McDonald replied. And he was. He had a habit of forgetting to lock his car and take the keys.

As they pulled out of the parking lot, Pep pulled out her pad and returned to the cipher.

KCAORE HTANAO EASUO HEAHT NIAUO AYTEA EMLLIAWI

The short break proved to be a good thing. It allowed Pep to take a fresh look at the cipher. Now she was seeing hidden words such as *core*, *tan*, *heat*, and *tea*. But she still couldn't put them together into a coherent sentence. Coke leaned over his sister's shoulder to check her progress.

Maybe the spaces between the words are just decoys, Pep thought as she took a piece of paper and a pencil out of her backpack. The spaces make it look as though those are separate words, but they may have been inserted within the letters to make it harder to decipher the message.

She rewrote the message, closing up the spaces.

KCAOREHTANAOEASUOHEAHTNIAUOAYTEAEMLLIAWI

It didn't make it any clearer.

"Maybe it's in another language," Coke whispered. "It looks like it might be Hawaiian or something."

"Or it could be a transposition cipher," Pep mumbled to herself.

She wrote out the cipher again, but this time in reverse order.

I WAILL MEAET YAOU AIN THAE HOUSAE OAN ATHE ROACK

"There must be a mistake in there somewhere," Coke whispered.

"No!" Pep said. "Wait a minute! It must have nulls in it."

"Nulls?" Coke asked. "What's a null?"

"A fake letter," she told him. "A letter that doesn't mean anything."

"How do you know this stuff?"

"I just do," she replied. "I'll take out all the *A*s and see what happens."

Pep rewrote the message:

I WILL MEET YOU IN THE HOUSE ON THE ROCK

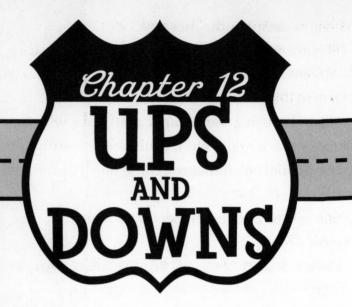

Chapter 12
UPS
AND
DOWNS

I WILL MEET YOU IN THE HOUSE ON THE ROCK

What the heck was *that* supposed to mean?

Pep looked at the words she had written.

"I never heard of a house on a rock," she whispered to her brother.

"There are probably *thousands* of houses that are built on rocks," Coke replied. "Maybe it's another secret message that means something completely different."

"These Genius Files people are so *annoying*," Pep complained. "Why don't they just tell us what's going on? Why do they have to make us figure it out?"

"The message didn't necessarily come from *them*,

y'know," Coke said. "It could have come from anybody."

"Then who are we supposed to meet in the house on the rock?" Pep asked, knowing she wasn't going to get an answer. "And when? This message doesn't tell us anything."

"We'll just have to keep our eyes open," Coke said, ending the discussion.

Dr. McDonald hopped on Route 101 North through the city and picked up Interstate 80 East as the RV crossed over the San Francisco–Oakland Bay Bridge. They were on their way now. If they wanted to, they could just stay on I-80 all the way across the country.

"Just fifteen hundred and forty-seven miles until we get to the largest ball of twine in the world!" Mrs. McDonald said excitedly after punching the data into her laptop. "And twenty-seven hundred and sixty-two miles to Washington."

2762

Want to follow the McDonalds on their cross-country trip? Get on the internet and go to Google Maps (http://maps.google.com), Mapquest (www.mapquest.com), Rand McNally (www.randmcnally.com), or whatever navigation website you like best.

Go ahead, I'll wait.

Okay, now type in BURLINGAME, CALIFORNIA (where the Museum of Pez Memorabilia is located), and click SEARCH MAPS. Click the little + or – sign on the screen to zoom in or out until you get a sense of where the twins are. Now you can follow them on their journey.

Pep did a quick mental calculation. If they averaged sixty-five miles per hour, it would take them more than forty-two hours to drive to Washington. That would be without stopping, of course. Once you add in sleeping, eating, stopping for gas, and just getting out to stretch their legs, it would be closer to . . . Oh, she didn't want to think about it.

And then, after they got to Washington and went to the wedding, they would have to drive that whole way back home, too.

> Go to Google Maps (http://maps.google.com/).
>
> Click Get Directions.
>
> In the A box, type Burlingame CA.
>
> In the B box, type Chico CA.
>
> Click Get Directions.

It was going to be a *long* summer.

Pep was already bored, and the trip had just begun. Coke turned on his iPod and got lost in the music as he mindlessly shuffled the deck of playing cards Bones had given them.

The McDonalds were cruising along I-80 for a little more than fifty miles when they started to see signs for Leisure Town and Nut Tree Airport. Dr. McDonald pulled onto Interstate 505 North.

"Where are you going, Dad?" Coke asked. "Why did you get off I-80?"

"Ask your mother," Dr. McDonald grumbled.

"We're going to the National Yo-Yo Museum!" Mrs. McDonald exclaimed. "It's only about two hours from here!"

"We're driving two hours out of our way to look at some *yo-yos*?" Coke asked, slapping himself on the forehead.

Not just *some* yo-yos. *Hundreds* of yo-yos. Glow-in-the-dark yo-yos. See-through yo-yos. Flintstone yo-yos and *Star Wars* yo-yos. The National Yo-Yo Museum has everything from antique 1920s yo-yos to today's metal alloy yo-yos with a centrifugal clutch transaxle, whatever *that* is.

Mrs. McDonald gasped as the family walked inside The Bird in Hand, an educational toy store in Chico, California, where the National Yo-Yo Museum is located. This was her kind of place.

"Feast your eyes, kids," Mrs. McDonald said, pulling out her camera to document the majesty of it all. "You're standing in front of the world's largest wooden yo-yo!"

It was a monster of a thing. 256 pounds. The string, unrolled, was seventy-five feet long. A little plaque on the floor said that "Big-Yo" was only used a few times. Once it was dropped off a crane over San Francisco Bay.

"The world's largest Pez dispenser is bigger," Coke said, unimpressed.

He knew all about yo-yos, of course, having once seen an article about them while he was bagging up the newspapers for recycling. He told the family that the yo-yo was invented in China, and the Greeks had them way back in 500 BCE.

"Fascinating," Dr. McDonald said sarcastically. "I hope this 'museum' doesn't get any government funding."

"This is real history, Dad!" Coke told his father. "Y'know, legend has it that Filipino hunters would hide in trees and hunt animals by bonking them on their heads with yo-yos from above. And during the French Revolution, people who were about to be guillotined would ease their tension by playing with yo-yos."

"I know that if they were about to chop off *my* head," Dr. McDonald replied, "I would want to use that time to play with a toy on a string."

The kids watched videos of people doing insane yo-yo tricks. There were some sample yo-yos on display, and Coke and Pep tried to do the tricks—with limited success.

After a short time, the kids had enough yo-yoing. They went out to the parking lot looking for something to do while Mrs. McDonald conducted her yo-yo research for *Amazing but True*. Their dad had left the RV door unlocked, as usual, so Coke went in and grabbed the Frisbee that Bones had given him. He held it out to Pep.

"I don't want to," Pep told her brother. "I don't know how."

"In a few days, you're gonna be thirteen years old," Coke told his sister. "It's about time you learned how to throw a Frisbee. It's a life skill everybody should have."

He handed her the disc, backed up ten yards, and urged her to give it a try. She flung it wildly, of course, curving it off to the side and almost hitting a parked car.

"Hold it *level*," Coke instructed as he ran off to retrieve the Frisbee. "Don't just use your arm. Put your whole body into it. And snap your wrist. Like *this*."

He made a perfect return toss, which Pep dropped.

"One more time," he encouraged her.

Pep tried to do as her brother said, and proceeded

to fling the Frisbee high into a grove of trees next to the parking lot.

"You are totally pathetic, you know that?" Coke told his sister. "C'mon, help me find it."

They ran into the woods and started poking around. A white Frisbee should not be hard to find in a grove of green trees. But it wasn't there. Or, at least, it wasn't within sight.

"It's got to be right *here*," Pep said. "I saw it go into the trees."

"You owe me ten bucks to get a new one," Coke told her.

"I do not," she replied. "You didn't pay for that Frisbee. Bones gave it to you."

At that moment, the twins walked around a thick maple tree. There was a rustling noise from above and then suddenly everything went dark. Something had fallen on their heads.

"What the—"

It was a large plastic tarp, the kind that people put under their tent when they go camping. Somebody grabbed them and wrapped two big arms around the tarp to prevent them from getting away.

"Shhhh! Quiet!" a man's voice warned.

"Help!" Pep tried to yell, but the sound was muffled by the tarp over her face.

"Keep your mouths shut and you won't be hurt," the man barked.

The twins struggled for a few seconds, but soon it became obvious that it was hopeless, and they stopped fighting. That's when their assailant pulled the tarp up over their heads and revealed himself.

It was Bones.

The McDonald twins gasped.

"Is *this* what you were looking for?" a woman's voice said.

The twins gasped a second time when they saw who was standing behind Bones with a Frisbee in her hand. It was Mya, the woman in red who had saved their lives when they were being chased on the cliff by the men in golf carts!

"You're . . . alive?" Pep asked, her eyes wide with wonder.

"We thought you died when the building exploded!" Coke told Bones.

"I was down in the basement," Bones said. "All I got was a flesh wound."

"Aren't all wounds flesh wounds?" Coke asked. "What else would you wound besides flesh?"

"We thought that dart killed you, Mya!" Pep said, hugging her. "We thought you died in our arms!"

"The poison wore off in a few minutes," Mya

123

informed them. "I was fine. I returned your back-packs to school for you."

Pep thought back and remembered what had happened at the cliff moments after Mya collapsed. Suddenly, she turned around and punched her brother in the stomach.

"*Oooof!*" Coke exclaimed. "Are you crazy? What did you do *that* for?"

"Because you pushed me off that cliff!" his sister yelled.

"I was trying to save your life!" Coke yelled back at her.

"Even if they hit me with one of those dart things, I would have survived!" Pep yelled again. "Mya survived! You didn't have to push me! We didn't have to go over that cliff!"

"Okay, okay, I'm sorry!" Coke said, rubbing his sore stomach. "How was I supposed to know that? She looked pretty dead to me. I had to make a snap decision. Give me a break!"

Bones stepped between the angry twins.

"You did the right thing pushing your sister off the cliff," he told Coke. "If you two had been captured up there, you would not be alive today. I'm quite sure of that."

"Look, we don't have time for pleasantries," Mya

interrupted. "I'm sure your parents are wondering where you are. We have important information for you."

"Is it about a house on a rock?"

"What?" Bones replied. "What house on a rock?"

"Didn't you put an envelope under my pillow last night with a coded message about meeting you in a house on a rock?" Coke asked.

"No," Bones replied. "You must be confusing me with the tooth fairy."

"Listen carefully," Mya said. "We found something out that is crucial to your survival. Some of the people who were involved in The Genius Files have abandoned our cause and now actively oppose us and the program that Dr. Warsaw created. Your health teacher, Mrs. Higgins, is one of them. There are others."

"Those bowler dudes," Pep said.

"Right," said Mya. "We don't know why these people are trying to kill you. But we're going to find out."

"How about finding out *fast*?" Coke said. "Before they actually *do* kill us?"

"We're trying our hardest," Bones told him. "In the meantime, we have your first mission. We intercepted a text message late last night. There is going to be a terrorist attack."

"Where?" Coke asked.

"In the United States," Mya said.

"Can you be more vague?" Coke asked.

"It will be at the site of the largest ball of twine in the world," said Mya.

"We're going there!" Pep exclaimed. "Our mother has this weird website called *Amazing but True*, and she's—"

"We know," said Bones.

"How do you know?" asked Coke.

"You'd be surprised at how much we know," Mya replied.

"But that's crazy!" Pep said. "Who would attack the largest ball of twine in the world?"

"The largest cat in the world?" suggested Coke.

"I didn't say they're necessarily going to attack the ball of twine," Bones told them. "All we know is, there will be an attack at the *site* of the ball of twine."

"What are they gonna do?" Coke asked.

"We don't know," Bones said.

"When are they gonna do it?" Coke asked.

"We don't know that either," Bones said.

"How come you know so much about *us*," Pep asked, "but you don't know anything about *them*?"

"We know they're trying to kill you," Mya said, "and they won't stop until they're successful, or until we kill them."

"So what are our instructions?" Coke asked.

"Simple. Stop the attack," Bones replied.

"Why can't *you* stop the attack?" Pep asked.

"We'll try to get there also," Mya said, "but there are other Genius Files children we are monitoring. We can't be everywhere at all times."

"How are we supposed to stop the attack?" Pep asked. "All we know is where it will be. We don't know when. We don't know how—"

"I'm sure you'll think of something," Bones interrupted her. "You're geniuses, right? That's why you were chosen."

"We must leave," Mya said. "Not a word of this to anyone."

Chapter 13
THE SECOND CIPHER

"Where *were* you kids?" Dr. McDonald asked anxiously when the twins came running back to the RV in the parking lot. "Your mother and I have been looking all over for you."

Pep turned to her brother.

"We were playing Frisbee," he explained. "Pep chucked it into the woods, and we had to go look for it. She totally can't throw."

"You can't catch!" his sister complained.

"Can too."

"Can not."

Dr. McDonald preferred to avoid arguments, especially the can too–can not variety. He opened his road atlas and flipped to the map of Nevada.

"Well, thank goodness you're safe!" Mrs. McDonald told the twins, reaching for her purse. "Five more minutes and we were going to call the police. Here, I bought you each a souvenir."

"Let me guess," Coke said. "Yo-yos?"

"How did you know?" Mrs. McDonald asked.

"I'm a genius."

Mrs. McDonald took two new yo-yos out of her purse: a red one for Coke and a blue one for Pep.

"Awesome!" Coke said. "Wanna see me walk the dog?"

"Maybe later," Mrs. McDonald replied. "Let's blow this pop stand."

"Mom," Pep said, "I wish you wouldn't buy this stuff. You're wasting your hard-earned money."

"Yeah, money doesn't grow on trees, Mom," Coke said as he tried to duplicate a yo-yo trick he had seen on the video.

"But you've *got* to bring home souvenirs!" Mrs. McDonald told them. "That's part of the fun of traveling!"

She passed around sandwiches she had made while the twins were in the woods. Dr. McDonald started the RV and pulled out of the parking lot. After driving a little Honda for years, he wasn't used to such a big

Go to Google Maps (http://maps.google .com/).

Click Get Directions.

In the A box, type Chico CA.

In the B box, type Truckee CA.

Click Get Directions.

vehicle, and he backed out carefully.

As he pulled onto Route 70 South, he relaxed a bit and began humming the old Willie Nelson song "On the Road Again." It wasn't long before they had merged back onto I-80, heading east.

"I was looking at the map," Dr. McDonald told the family after they had been on the road for a while. "Lake Tahoe is only about an hour from here. That might be a good place for us to stop for the night. Maybe we can even stay for a day or two. We could go swimming or kayaking. Have some fun, you know? Lake Tahoe is beautiful."

"No!" Pep shouted.

"We want to go see the largest ball of twine in the world!" shouted Coke.

"Yeah," Pep added. "Lakes are a big bore."

Mrs. McDonald turned around in the front seat.

"Wait a minute," she said. "Yesterday everybody was making fun of me for wanting to go see the largest ball of twine in the world. And now you're all anxious to get there. What's going on?"

"Yeah," Dr. McDonald said. "Why are you suddenly so interested in that silly ball of twine?"

As usual, Pep looked to Coke for the answer. She wasn't about to tell her parents that there would be some sort of attack at the ball of twine and that they had to help stop it.

Coke thought fast.

"We're twins," he announced. "And *twine* is *twin* with an *e* at the end. So we want to see it."

"That's ridiculous!" Dr. McDonald sputtered. "So instead of swimming and kayaking on a beautiful lake, you want to go look at a ball of twine because it has an *E* in it?"

"Yes!" the twins agreed.

"You wouldn't understand," Pep said. "You're not a twin."

"Well, I'm pleased to see you kids are getting into the spirit of the trip," Mrs. McDonald said. "The twine ball is in Cawker City, Kansas."

"Then that's where we want to go," Coke declared. "We hate swimming and kayaking."

"Since when?" his father asked. "You used to *love* swimming and kayaking when you were little."

"Please, please, please, please?" begged Pep.

Dr. McDonald could not resist a child with puppy dog eyes, especially when it was his own. He sighed

when the exit for Lake Tahoe appeared on the side of the road, and he drove right by it.

Mrs. McDonald passed her laptop back to the kids so they could see the route to Kansas. The McDonalds would have to drive along I-80 all the way across Nevada, through the top of Utah, across the southern part of Wyoming, and halfway across Nebraska before detouring south into Kansas.

1414

"It says Cawker City is 1,414 miles from here," Mrs. McDonald informed the family, "and today is June nineteenth. It should take us a few days to get there, depending on how often we stop."

"Speaking of which, I'm beat," Dr. McDonald announced. "Let's start looking for a campground."

About ten miles from the Nevada border, signs began to appear at the side of the road: DONNER LAKE . . . DONNER PASS ROAD . . . DONNER MEMORIAL STATE PARK . . . DONNER CAMP PICNIC AREA . . .

"The Donner Party!" Pep yelled excitedly, almost causing her dad to drive off the road. "This is where they were!"

Ever since she was little, for reasons nobody could quite explain, Pep had been fascinated by the Donner Party. Other girls become obsessed with soccer, dolls, scrapbooking, or some boy band. But Pep loved the Donner Party.

She was probably the only child in America who knew the story. In 1846, George Donner and his brother Jacob, Illinois farmers, set out for the promise of California in covered wagons with several families, including their own. They took a shortcut that turned out to be a longer route, hit bad weather, ran out of food, and resorted to cannibalism (yes, that means eating each other). Only a few members of the party survived.

Some party, huh?

Dr. McDonald spotted a sign for a campground in the town of Truckee, California, so he pulled off the highway.

"Maybe they have a Donner Party museum here," Pep said hopefully.

"Donner Party museum?" Coke said, snorting. "Are you kidding? Nobody's gonna make a museum about a bunch of cannibals."

"Why not?" Pep asked. "Somebody made a museum about a bunch of yo-yos. Somebody made a museum about a bunch of Pez dispensers. Why not a museum devoted to the memory of the Donner Party?"

That's when they saw a sign at the side of the road.

Visit
THE DONNER
PARTY EXHIBIT
at The Emigrant
Trail Museum

"See!" Pep hollered. "They *do* have a Donner Party museum! Can we go there? Please, Dad? Please, please, please?"

Dr. McDonald pulled into Donner Memorial State Park and found the museum parking lot.

"It *is* historical, I suppose," he said.

"I might be able to use this on *Amazing but True*," Mrs. McDonald added.

"I can imagine the souvenirs they sell in the gift shop," Coke remarked. "Do you think it has a meat department?"

The exhibit was actually pretty interesting. There was a twenty-five-minute video about the Donner Party and a musket that one of the desperate pioneers had used to shoot an eight-hundred-pound grizzly bear. Outside was a memorial that showed how high the snow had gotten that tragic winter: twenty-two feet.

"I'm not entirely sure that museum was appropriate for children," Mrs. McDonald said when the family piled back inside the RV.

"The Donner Party were heroes," Pep said. "They did what they had to do to survive."

"Yeah, lighten up, Mom," Coke agreed. "Cannibals are cool."

"It *was* educational," Dr. McDonald admitted.

"Because of what happened to the Donner Party, Californians sent relief teams with food and water for people who were heading west during the gold rush a couple of years later. So in the long run, they saved a lot of lives."

After a few wrong turns, the McDonalds found a campground where they could spend the night. They had driven more than two hundred miles, almost all the way across California. Mrs. McDonald baked some freeze-dried chicken in the RV's little microwave oven, and the family eagerly wolfed it down while sitting at a picnic table next to their campsite.

"Do you want me to do a dump here, Dad?" Coke asked, remembering that his chore for the trip was to empty the holding tank below the toilet.

"No, we can wait a few days for that," Dr. McDonald replied. "Let the tank fill up a little."

It was a simple campground. Once the sun went down, there wasn't a whole lot to do. Without any wood to make a campfire, the McDonalds climbed into their four sleeping nooks and curled up with books. One by one, they dropped off to sleep.

Around three o'clock in the morning, a man wearing a black suit and a bowler hat tiptoed over to the RV. He had a piece of paper with him, about three inches by seven inches, which he carefully slipped

under the left windshield wiper. Then he crept away silently in the night.

This is what it said on the piece of paper:

JNTET FFHNO LCDNB LTYUL
VSEED NTHTU EWNYI TOECO
KOTEA EORIEDPNOITOR

Chapter 14
THE
SINGING
SAND

The twins woke up the next morning—June 20—to hear their father ranting to nobody in particular.

"A ticket?" Dr. McDonald bellowed. "I can't believe the cops gave me a parking ticket. In a campground! That's un-American!"

Coke buried his face in his pillow and tried to go back to sleep.

When Dr. McDonald went outside and peeled the "ticket" off the windshield, he realized it wasn't a ticket at all. No ticket would say

JNTET FFHNO LCDNB LTYUL
VSEED NTHTU EWNYI TOECO
KOTEA EORIEDPNOITOR

"What do you make of this, Bridge?" he asked.

"It's not a ticket," Mrs. McDonald replied. "Maybe it's a new kind of sudoku puzzle or some word game. It looks like some sort of a code."

With the word *code*, Pep and Coke bolted up from their bunks. If somebody left a message with a secret code on the windshield, it was meant for *them*, not for their parents.

Coke ran outside in his pajamas and bare feet to snatch the piece of paper out of his father's hand. He glanced at it for a few seconds—long enough to commit it to memory. Then he ripped up the paper and threw the pieces in the garbage can at the side of their campsite.

"It's probably just some kids pulling a prank," he said. "So, what's for breakfast? And what fabulous place are we going to visit today? Maybe a museum devoted to Mr. Potato Head?"

"Oh, you'll see," his mother replied. "All I can tell you is this—it has something to do with singing."

While the others got dressed and brushed their teeth over the little sink, Coke carefully rewrote the message from the windshield on a sheet of paper. Even people who have photographic memories know that photos fade in time.

"Somebody left us another cipher," he confirmed

to his sister while their parents prepared breakfast. "If it's anything like the last one, you should be able to solve it."

Pep looked at the letters and then wrote them down in reverse order on her pad, the same way she did with the first cipher. Only this time the message didn't make any sense. It didn't look anything like English.

"What's wrong?" Coke asked his sister after she had been staring at the pad for five minutes.

"Nothing," she replied. "It's just a different kind of cipher. Give me a little time. I'll crack it."

When everyone had eaten and the dishes were washed, Dr. McDonald started the RV and jumped back onto I-80 heading east. In about an hour they crossed the state line.

> Go to Google Maps (http://maps.google.com/).
>
> Click Get Directions.
>
> In the A box, type Truckee CA.
>
> In the B box, type Fallon NV.
>
> Click Get Directions.

"Did you guys know that the word *nevada* means 'snowcapped' in Spanish?" Coke announced.

Welcome to
NEVADA
The Silver State

"Very impressive!" Mrs. McDonald said.

"Thank you, Mr. Show-off," said Pep.

Less than ten miles from the California border is the big city of Reno. The flashing lights of the casinos were beckoning, but Dr. McDonald barely glanced at them.

"Hey, gambling is legal here, Dad," Coke hollered from the backseat. "We should hit the slots. Play some blackjack."

"You're too young to gamble," Dr. McDonald hollered back, "and I'm too smart."

Coke shared a smile with his sister. They had been attacked by guys in golf carts with blow guns, jumped off a cliff, been locked in a burning school, and had their heads stapled, but putting coins in a slot machine was considered too dangerous for kids. Go figure.

As the buildings of Reno disappeared behind them, Pep worked feverishly on the cipher. She jumbled the letters on her pad every which way, trying to make sense of them. She grew increasingly frustrated.

The family continued east on I-80; and shortly after passing Wadsworth, Nevada, the road split. Mrs. McDonald instructed her husband to take the Reno Highway, which is also called Route 50 East. It wasn't long before they reached the town of Fallon and a sign . . .

They had driven another twenty-five miles east when Mrs. McDonald suddenly shouted, "There it is!"

In the distance, nestled between two mountain ranges, out in the middle of nowhere, was a gigantic mountain of sand.

A beach at the edge of the ocean is no big deal. But a beach in the middle of Nevada was just plain strange.

To make things even stranger, as the McDonalds got closer, they could hear the sand *singing*.

Sand Mountain Recreation Area is famous out West because it gives off an odd, otherworldly moaning sound, like the soundtrack to a horror movie. Dr. McDonald pulled onto a dirt road that brought them to the edge of the dune. Theirs was the only vehicle in the parking lot.

Even the kids, who liked to pretend that nothing impressed them, climbed out of the RV to listen to the sand. A sign stuck in the ground read TAKE ONLY PHOTOS. LEAVE ONLY FOOTPRINTS.

The dune is two miles long and six hundred feet high. There was no sign of a human being for miles around, but the sand was talking, singing, moaning. Pep felt goose pimples on her arms. This was a noise she had never heard before.

"It sounds like somebody who's wounded," Dr. McDonald observed, "but not quite dead yet."

"It's because of the size of the grains of sand and the way the grains bump into each other," said Coke, who had once read an article on the topic in a science magazine while he was getting his hair cut.

Coke told the others that in order to "sing," the grains of sand have to be very dry, round, and polished; and they have to *move*, either because of the wind or some geological force. There are twenty-seven areas in the world where there are singing sand dunes, and only four of them are in the United States.

"I don't like that sound," Pep said quietly. "It's creepy."

"I think it's marvelous!" Mrs. McDonald gushed, reaching for her laptop. "I'm going to tell my readers all about it!"

"In that case, I'll be taking a snooze," Dr. McDonald said as he climbed into the RV and reclined the driver's seat back as far as it would go.

"Hey, you wanna hike up there?" Coke asked his sister. "I wonder what it sounds like at the top."

"No thanks," Pep replied.

"Come on, you afraid?"

"No, I'm not *afraid*," Pep insisted. "I just don't want to."

Coke proceeded to make chicken noises, which prompted Pep to start sprinting up the sand dune ahead of him.

"Last one to the summit is a rotten egg!" she yelled.

"You kids have fun," Dr. McDonald yelled after them. "The old fogies will stay in the RV and listen to the sand singing from the parking lot."

"Here," Mrs. McDonald said as she flipped a little glass jar to Coke, "fill this with sand from the summit. There's no gift shop here. You gotta bring home a souvenir."

He stuck the jar in his pocket and chased Pep up the steep slope of Sand Mountain.

As the twins climbed, they could hear the pitch of the "music" change and feel the vibrations in their bones. It was an eerie feeling. Coke looked up in the sky for a plane. It was hard to believe that the sound

he was hearing was made by the sand alone.

It was still morning, but the surface was already hot. They could feel the sand through their sneakers.

"We should have brought a water bottle," Pep said when they were halfway to the top, "and the Frisbee. This would be a good place to throw it."

"I don't want to chase your wild throws all over this mountain," Coke replied.

The sand was soft, and their feet sank into it with each step. They turned to wave at their parents down in the parking lot, but the RV was already a dot on the horizon. They were so far away.

"I know this is gonna sound crazy," Pep suddenly said, panting as she climbed, "but I have the feeling that somebody is following us."

"Oh, *please*," Coke replied. "Will you relax? How could somebody follow us? There's nobody around for miles. See? The parking lot is empty. Nobody's here but us."

As they neared the top of the mountain, Coke took out the jar his mother had given him. Pep got down on her hands and knees to help him fill it with sand.

Coke had just screwed on the top and stuck the jar in his pocket when he heard a voice. It wasn't the voice of the sand.

"Don't stand up," a man ordered.

The twins turned around quickly to look. There was a man standing about ten feet behind them. He was wearing a black suit and a black bowler hat. In his hand was a long, shiny sword. The sun reflected off of it.

"Who are *you*?" Pep asked, shielding her eyes from the glare. "How did you get up here?"

"Who I am or how I got up here is not important, sweetheart," the man told her.

"I know who you are!" said Coke, who recognized the man right away. "You're one of the guys in the golf carts! The dudes with the bowler hats and the blow guns."

"Very good," bowler dude said. "That was clever the way you two jumped off that cliff to get away from us the other day. It took me by surprise. But it won't happen again."

"What are you doing here?" Pep asked, squeezing her brother's hand tightly.

"I thought you were supposed to be so smart, sweetheart," the bowler dude said, holding up his sword. "It's obvious what I'm doing here. I'm going to kill you. You know what they say: if at first you don't succeed, try, try again. But I won't make the same mistake *this* time. No cliffs."

"You're going to kill us with a *sword*?" Coke asked.

"Of course not!" the bowler dude replied. "That would be . . . uncivilized. Come with me."

"What did we do?" Pep asked, tears in her eyes. "We didn't hurt anybody. We're just—"

"Shut up, sweetheart."

Holding the sword over their heads, the bowler dude marched the twins up to the very top of Sand Mountain and then a few yards farther, where there was a pit that had been dug into the dune on the other side. It was seven feet deep and about the size of a pool table.

"You'll die from dehydration," the bowler dude informed them. "It's far more humane."

"I'm not getting into that pit," Pep said defiantly.

"Me nei—"

The bowler dude held his sword sideways in front of him and used the flat side to shove both of them backward. They lost their balance and tumbled into the pit.

"Owwww!" Coke said, landing hard on his side. Pep popped up right away. She got on her tiptoes and jumped, half expecting Mya and Bones to suddenly show up and save them again. But the pit was too deep to see out of, and there was nobody else around, anyway.

"Your friends aren't here to help you *this* time,

sweetheart," the bowler dude told her. "My good friend Mrs. Higgins has taken care of them. They won't be saving your lives anymore."

"Help!" Pep screamed. "Mom! Dad! Help!"

"Save your energy, sweetheart. They can't hear you," the bowler dude told her. "The singing sand is drowning out your voice. That's why I chose this as the perfect spot to kill you."

"You'll never get away with this!" Pep shouted.

The bowler dude chuckled to himself.

"Without any water, your bodies won't be able to cool off. Your muscles will start cramping. You'll get heat exhaustion and then heat stroke. You'll feel dizzy and weak. Your temperatures will go up to 107 degrees. And then you'll die. Hey, do you kids play golf? Sand traps have been the graveyard of many great golfers. And now one will be yours."

He chuckled at his little joke.

"As soon as our parents realize we're missing, they'll be up here," Coke said. "They'll rescue us."

The bowler dude shook his head and laughed.

"Your parents are used to you two running off," he said. "By the time they get up here, you'll be dead. I'll simply cover your bodies with sand, and they'll find nothing. You will have vanished without a trace."

Pep was crying now. Coke was on the verge. He

looked around desperately for a way to get out of the pit.

"What did we ever do to *you*?" Pep sobbed.

"Nothing. I do what I'm told, sweetheart."

"By who?" Coke asked. "Who's paying you?"

"That's *my* business," the bowler dude said.

Coke eyed the sword in the bowler dude's hand. If only he could get hold of it.

"What's with you and the old-time weapons?" Coke asked. "Swords. Blow guns. What, are they afraid to trust you with a *real* gun?"

"I'm kickin' it old school," the bowler dude explained. "There was something elegant in the weapons before the age of gunpowder. Killing with guns and dropping bombs from planes is too easy."

"You're crazy!" Pep shouted through her tears.

The bowler dude ignored her. He took a plastic water bottle out of his pocket and made a little show of leaning his head back to drain it slowly.

"Pretty hot up here today, eh?" he said, tossing the empty bottle into the pit. "Must be over a hundred degrees."

"That's littering!" Pep hollered at him. "Don't you care about the environment?"

"Uh, I don't think that should be our highest priority right now," Coke told his sister.

"Don't worry; the bottle will decompose in a few hundred years," the bowler dude told them, "around the same time they find your bones. Ha-ha! They say life is the pits; but, in your case, *death* turned out to be the pits. So long, kiddies."

As he slid his sword into his belt and turned to walk away, Coke yelled, "Wait!"

He realized that this assassin was, ironically, the only person who could save them. If the bowler dude left, there would be no way to get out of the pit. As long as they were talking, there was a chance to survive.

"Did you send us a coded message?" Coke asked. "Something about meeting you at a house on a rock?"

"If I have something to say to you, I'll say it to your face," the bowler dude replied. "I don't send secret messages. Now, is there anything else you request? I'm a busy man."

"Yeah," Coke said, "could you help us out of this pit? We're kinda stuck down here."

The bowler dude laughed and clapped his hands. "I like that," he said. "You retain a sense of humor even as you are going to die. I'm sure that we would have become friends if I hadn't had to kill you. Ha-ha-ha!"

"I *told* you we should have brought the Frisbee," Pep said to her brother.

"Yeah, a lot of good that would have done."

"We could have thrown it at him," Pep said, "or something!"

Coke was going to insult his sister's Frisbee skills, but she had given him an idea. As the bowler dude turned to walk away again, Coke reached into his pocket. He pulled out the jar of sand he had collected for his mother. It was his only chance. He reared back, wound up, and heaved it at the bowler dude.

The jar hit him directly on the back of his head.

The bowler dude let out a brief yelp of pain and staggered backward a step. There was blood running down his neck. He went to put a hand on the wound, but it never got there. His knees buckled, and he fell backward and slid headfirst into the pit, next to the McDonald twins.

"Good throw!" Pep hollered.

"Quick! Grab his sword!" Coke said.

Coke was about to punch the bowler dude, but there was no need. He was *out*. The blow to the back of his head, combined with the fall into the pit, had knocked him unconscious. Pep grabbed the sword just to be on the safe side.

"Do you think he's dead?" she asked.

"What am I, a doctor?" Coke said. "Who cares if he's dead? Let's get out of here!"

There was just one problem. They couldn't climb out. The pit was too deep. When they tried to grab hold of the side and pull themselves up, they just got handfuls of sand. They tried making a foothold with their hands. They tried using the bowler dude's unconscious body as a step. Nothing worked.

"Try using the sword!" Pep said desperately.

"What? You want me to carve steps into the sand?"

"No, dope!" she replied, taking the sword herself.

Pep made a mark on the side of the pit about three feet above the bottom. Then she stabbed the sword into the wall, hard. It slid into the sand about a foot deep.

Coke realized what she had in mind. He put his weight against the handle of the sword and pushed it another foot or so into the side of the pit. It held firm, with not much more than the handle sticking out.

Coke hoisted up his sister. She carefully put one foot on the handle of the sword and climbed out of the pit. Then she reached down and helped Coke climb out. They looked into the pit one last time to see the bowler dude lying there, motionless.

"I've played in the sand enough for one day," Coke said.

"Yeah," she agreed. "Let's blow this pop stand."

When they finally got back down to the parking lot, their parents were waiting impatiently.

"What took you so long?" Mrs. McDonald asked. "You were up there for a long time."

"Did you kids have fun?" Dr. McDonald asked. "What was it like up there? Did it sound different?"

"It was *scary*, Mom," Pep said. "Real scary."

"Did you remember to fill the jar with sand?" Mrs. McDonald asked.

"Uh . . . yeah," Coke replied weakly.

"So, where is it?"

"I . . . guess I left it up there," Coke said honestly.

"How could you leave it there?" his mother asked, exasperated. "What is your problem? I swear, I can't understand you kids. I don't ask a lot. I ask you to do one simple thing. . . ."

"Can we just get out of here?" Pep requested. She wasn't about to tell her mother that they used her souvenir to bonk a guy on the head and very possibly kill him.

They piled back into the RV and drove away, serenaded by the sound of the singing sand in the distance.

Chapter 15
I'LL BE WATCHING YOU

As the McDonalds drove back on Lovelock High-way up to I-80, the twins sat without saying a word. Suddenly they realized how naive they had been. They had thought that once they'd gotten on the road with their parents, their troubles would be over. They had thought they would be safe in the RV. Who could bother them in the deserts of Nevada? Their parents would protect them.

Right.

Coke felt the back of his head. There was a GPS chip buried in there somewhere, he remembered. Bones had staple gunned it into his scalp. But who knew where Bones was now? He didn't show up at the sand dune to help them. That bowler dude guy had said that Mrs. Higgins had "taken care of" their friends. Maybe Bones and Mya weren't even alive anymore.

Coke looked out the window at the big sky. Mrs. Higgins was working with those bowler dudes to kill him and Pep. That much he knew. Maybe satellites were tracking their position, following their every move, listening in on every conversation.

What had they gotten themselves into?

He fiddled with his deck of cards as these thoughts were running through his brain. The cards had become his security blanket in a way. Just holding them calmed him. Pep sat with her eyes closed. She was shaken, traumatized by the incident at the top of Sand Mountain.

Dr. McDonald pulled on to I-80 and announced that his goal was to make it across Nevada by the end of the day. It would be about 320 miles.

320

"How about a travel game to pass the time?" Mrs. McDonald piped up cheerfully. "I'll name

Go to Google Maps (http://maps.google.com/).

Click Get Directions.

In the A box, type Toulon NV.

In the B box, type Wendover UT.

Click Get Directions.

a place, and you guys have to think of a different place that starts with the last letter of my place. Got it? I'll start. Vietnam."

"Miami," said Dr. McDonald.

"Islip," said Mrs. McDonald. "It's a city in New York State."

"Punjab," said Dr. McDonald. "It's a region in India."

"What about you kids?" Mrs. McDonald hollered behind her. "Don't you want to play? Get into the spirit of it! Can you think of a place that starts with the letter *B*?"

"Boring," said Coke.

He was right, too. There actually is a town in Oregon called Boring. Go ahead and look it up.

"We don't want to play right now, Mom," Pep said quietly. "We're tired."

"You kids are no fun at all," Mrs. McDonald said.

She gave up the idea of playing a travel game and slipped a CD out of the visor in front of her—*The Best of Police*. The first song began to play. A guy was singing about how he would always be watching somebody—every breath they take, every move they make.

The song sent a shiver down Pep's spine. Somebody *was* watching them. She took out her cell phone and punched in a text to her brother. . . .

155

```
PEP: U think that bowler dude on sand mountain
is dead?
COKE: Don't no. Don't wanna no. Probly not.
PEP: We couldve killed him. The sword was just
lying there.
COKE: Coulda shoulda woulda.
PEP: If hes still alive he could bother us
again.
COKE: I no.
```

Pep pulled out her pad and pencil to resume work on the unsolvable cipher they had found on the windshield that morning.

JNTET FFHNO LCDNB LTYUL VSEED NTHTU EWNYI TOECO KOTEA EORIEDPNOITOR

She tried reading every second letter to see if it made any sense that way. Then she tried reading every third letter, and then every fourth letter. Then she tried them all backward. It was just gibberish. She closed her eyes again.

People who have never been to Nevada tend to think it's just a barren desert with two big cities: Las Vegas and Reno. In fact, it's the most mountainous state in the nation and is filled with jagged canyons, lush valleys, gorgeous fields of alfalfa hay, sheep ranches, and cactus. *Lots* of cactus. And yes, the occasional rattlesnake, Gila monster, and kangaroo rat.

There are also a lot of cool places in Nevada, especially for people who gravitate toward the offbeat.

Like Coke and Pep's mom.

Mrs. McDonald reached into her tote bag full of guidebooks and pulled out one titled *Eccentric America*.

"Hey, in Middlegate they have this thing called the Nevada Shoe Tree," she announced. "It says here that some couple was about to get married and the groom was afraid his bride was going to run away, so he threw her shoes up into the tree. Lots of other people threw their shoes up there too, and today that tree is filled with shoes. We should go there."

"Middlegate is a hundred miles south of here," Dr. McDonald said. "I'm not driving that far out of our way to see a tree with shoes on it."

"You're no fun," Mrs. McDonald said. "Hey, here's something that's only about five miles off the highway, outside of Imlay. It's called Thunder Mountain."

"Is it an amusement park?" Pep asked.

"No," her mother replied, "a Creek Indian named Chief Rolling Mountain Thunder built a house out of concrete, old car bodies, and lots of other stuff

he found lying around. The top floor is made out of bottles, and the windows are made from car windshields."

"That sounds cool," Coke remarked.

"It sounds like a waste of time to me," Dr. McDonald said bluntly. "I thought you were all so anxious to see that ridiculous ball of twine in Kansas."

"Yeah!" Pep said, suddenly remembering. "Let's drive straight through to Kansas. We want to go to the ball of twine."

She shot a look at her brother. No words were necessary. They both remembered that they had a mission to accomplish. Somebody was going to pull off an attack at the largest ball of twine in the world. Neither of them wanted to get out of the RV until they got there. Neither of them wanted to repeat what happened on Sand Mountain.

"Well, we have to stop *here*," Dr. McDonald said to the others as he pulled off at an exit marked BATTLE MOUNTAIN. "We need to gas up. And how about we eat lunch out today?"

He pulled into the parking lot of a fast-food joint. The twins got out of the RV cautiously. They looked around for any sign of guys with bowler hats, blow guns, and golf carts; or psychotic health teachers; or other suspicious characters. Not seeing anything out of the ordinary, they relaxed a bit. Dr. McDonald led the family into the restaurant. The sign said SEAT YOURSELF, and they slid into a booth. The waitress, an older woman, came over with menus.

"Welcome to Battle Mountain," she said cheerfully, "the Armpit of America."

"That's not a very nice thing to say about your own town," Mrs. McDonald said with a laugh.

"Honey," the waitress said, "it's our claim to fame."

It was true. She told the McDonalds that back in 2001, *The Washington Post* had named Battle Mountain, Nevada, the Armpit of America. Instead of being humiliated over it, the town had convinced the company that makes Old Spice deodorant to sponsor an annual Festival in the Pit. They had featured events such as antiperspirant tossing and an armpit beauty pageant. But those festivities had "dried out" a few years back.

"Bummer," Coke said. "Too bad we missed that."

"That's what I love about America," Mrs. McDonald said, taking notes for her website. "You never know what you're going to find."

The burgers were greasy but good. Then it was back onto I-80. Soon there were signs for Elko, Nevada, where the National Cowboy Poetry Gathering is held each year. That's right, cowboys and cowgirls come

from all over the world to recite poetry. Mrs. McDonald suggested they stop and try to meet some cowboys there, but the sun was getting low in the sky and Dr. McDonald wanted to press on.

Small Nevada towns passed by: Osino . . . Halleck . . . Deeth . . . and even a town called Welcome. Continuing down the highway, with darkness falling, they crossed the state line.

Welcome to
UTAH
The Beehive State

"Woo-hoo!" Coke yelled, clapping his hands. "Did you know that it's illegal to hunt whales in Utah? That's pretty strange, considering it's landlocked."

Mrs. McDonald smiled to herself. It was nice to know that her son shared her fascination with useless information.

"Nobody cares, Coke," Pep told her brother. "How

many miles to the largest ball of twine in the world?"

Mrs. McDonald punched it into her laptop.

"Nine hundred and eighty-seven miles!" she announced.

"Woo-hoo!"

They had to drive a few miles before they saw signs for a campground that allowed RVs. Coke asked his dad if he should do a dump before they went to sleep, but it was decided to wait a few days until the level in the holding tank was higher. They all changed into pj's and crawled into their little beds.

Before she turned off her light, Pep took one last look at the cipher that had been in the back of her mind all day.

JNTET FFHNO LCDNB LTYUL VSEED NTHTU EWNYI TOECO KOTEA EORIEDPNOITOR

She was stumped. Frustrated after a few minutes, she gave up and slipped the pad under her mattress. She flipped off the little light and went to sleep.

If you ever woke up in the middle of the night with an idea or a vivid dream, you know that the human brain doesn't just turn on and off like a light. It keeps thinking even when you're sleeping. It is an amazing machine.

Just before dawn, Pep awoke with an idea. She got out of bed and shook Coke until he opened his eyes.

"I got it!" she whispered in his ear. "I think it might be a rail fence cipher!"

"A what?" Coke rubbed his eyes. "Are you crazy? You'll wake Mom and Dad. Go back to sleep."

"No, I need your help."

Pep reached for her pad and wrote out the cipher again with no spaces between the "words," this time dividing the letters into two rows.

JNTETFFHNOLCDNBLTYULVSEEDNTHT
UEWNYITOECOKOTEAEORIEDPNOITOR

Next she wrote down the first letter of the top line: *J.* Then she wrote down the first letter of the bottom line: *U.* The second letter of the top line: *N.* The second letter of the bottom line: *E.*

JUNE

Now she was getting somewhere! With her brother fully awake and whispering in her ear, Pep kept writing down letters, alternating between the top line and the bottom line. It didn't take long to work out the entire message that way.

JUNETWENTYFIFTHONEOCLOCKDONTBELATEYOUR-
LIVESDEPENDONITTHOTR

And when she added spaces where they seemed to fit . . .

JUNE TWENTY FIFTH ONE OCLOCK DONT BE LATE YOUR LIVES DEPEND ON IT THOTR

"*THOTR*?" whispered Coke. "What's *THOTR*? That part must be a mistake."

"No, it's like a signature," his sister whispered back. "THOTR must be the person who's been sending us these messages!"

They looked at the letters *THOTR* carefully. They didn't look as if they were anybody's name. The word *hot* was in there. *Hotter*? *Other*? *Throttle*? *Otter*? Pep switched the letters around, looking for words that might fit. *TROT. TO. TOT. ROT. HOT TO TROT*?

And then, simultaneously, they both figured out what *THOTR* meant.

"The house on the rock!"

Mr. and Mrs. McDonald nearly woke up from the noise.

"*THOTR* stands for 'the house on the rock'!" Pep

said. "We need to be there at one o'clock on June twenty-fifth. That's our birthday!"

"It's also four days from now," Coke informed her.

"But we don't even know where this stupid house is," Pep said. "It could be *anywhere*. How are we supposed to find it?"

"Beats me."

Chapter 16
DADS GONE WILD

Coke and Pep leaned over the message, staring at it as if the words might change if they looked at them hard enough.

"What is it with this house on a rock?" Coke whispered.

"I don't know," his sister replied. "But we have to figure it out. Somebody wants us to be there on our birthday."

"And don't forget; we need to get to the ball of twine, too," Coke noted. "We promised Bones."

With so much on their minds, the twins went back to bed but slept poorly. They were groggy when their father woke them up early. He seemed anxious to check out of the campground and get on the road.

Northern Utah didn't look much different from the eastern part of Nevada. Flat. Hot. Dry. There wasn't a whole lot to look at, at least not along I-80. It was going to be one of those staring-out-the-window kind of days.

After a few miles, a sign appeared.

Bonneville Salt Flats STATE PARK

Dr. McDonald veered off the highway at exit 4.

"Ben, where are you going?" Mrs. McDonald asked.

"You'll see."

He drove a few miles into the state park without saying a word to anybody. Mrs. McDonald and the twins shot nervous glances at one another. It wasn't like Dr. Benjamin McDonald to do impulsive, spontaneous things. He was a planner. He liked schedules and lists.

"*This* is a state park?" Pep asked, looking at the scenery. "It doesn't look like any state park I ever saw."

"Yeah, what's so great about *this* place, Dad?" Coke asked. "There are lots of cooler state parks we could go to. This place looks like a lot of nothing."

"A lot of *salt*," Mrs. McDonald added.

"That's *exactly* what it is," Dr. McDonald agreed, smiling as he pulled off the access road and onto the white salt flat itself. "Thirty thousand acres of salt. Nothing but salt."

"And we came here for *what* reason exactly?" Pep asked.

"Do you have a sodium deficiency in your diet, Dad?" Coke asked.

"Look around you," Dr. McDonald told the family. "It's so flat here that you can almost see the curvature of the earth. It's so barren, even the simplest forms of life can't survive. It's like another planet, an alien world of potassium, magnesium lithium, and sodium chloride."

The twins looked at each other. There was a good chance that their father had lost his marbles.

"Thousands of years ago," he continued, "Lake Bonneville covered a third of what is now Utah. When the lake evaporated, salt and minerals were left on

167

the bottom. And over time, the surface became flat and hard."

"Okay, can we go now?" Pep said, shielding her eyes from the blinding sun reflecting off the salt flat. "It's probably a hundred degrees. If the RV broke down, we could die out here."

"Yeah, this place is lame, Dad," Coke added.

"This place is for *me*," Dr. McDonald said dreamily. "You get to go to your yo-yo museums and your Pez museums. You get to see your giant ball of twine and all those other goofball places Mom wants to visit. The Bonneville Salt Flats is a place I always wanted to go to ever since I was a little boy."

"Why, Ben?" Mrs. McDonald asked. "What's here? Is this some sort of midlife crisis for you?"

"Yes, it is," Dr. McDonald admitted. "Do you guys know what the Bonneville Salt Flats is famous for?"

"I do," Coke replied.

Of course, Coke knew all about the Bonneville Salt Flats from a Saturday morning TV special he'd seen years earlier. He remembered every detail.

It turns out that back in 1914, a daredevil named Teddy Tezlaff brought an early car—a Blitzen Benz— out to the Bonneville Salt Flats and drove it 141.73 miles per hour: the world record at the time. Ever since then car buffs from all over the world have come to the salt flats to see how fast they could drive. Over the years they bumped the world land speed record up to 300 mph, then 400 mph, and eventually past 600 mph.

"When I was a kid," Dr. McDonald told the family, "this guy named Craig Breedlove brought a jet-powered car out here and broke the six-hundred-mile-per-hour barrier. I still remember the name of his car: *Spirit of America*. Ever since then, I wanted to come to Bonneville."

"I understand, Ben," Mrs. McDonald said, patting his shoulder. "So we're going to watch a race here?"

"No," he replied. "Same sentence. Take out the 'watch a.'"

"We're going to *race* here?" Pep asked, alarmed.

"That's right," Dr. McDonald said. He had a devilish gleam in his eyes, and he gripped the steering wheel tightly.

"Are you out of your mind, Ben?" his wife asked.

"We're going to see how fast this baby can go," Dr. McDonald said calmly.

"Yeah, let's do it, Dad!" urged Coke.

"This is insanity," Pep said.

"It's a recreational vehicle, Ben!" Mrs. McDonald said urgently. "An RV isn't designed for racing."

"Going fast is one of man's most primal desires,"

Dr. McDonald said, staring at the salt flat ahead of him. "This will be my only chance to ever do this. Fasten your seat belts."

With that, he hit the gas pedal.

The wheels spun at first on the salt, but soon they got a grip and the RV lurched forward. They were all slammed backward into their seats.

"Ben, you're going to damage the RV!" Mrs. McDonald yelled.

"It's okay!" he shouted back. "It's a rental!"

After a sluggish start, the RV started picking up speed. *Fifty, sixty, seventy miles per hour.* With nothing around for miles and miles, Dr. McDonald didn't have to worry about roads, stop signs, guardrails, traffic lights, pedestrians, or police cars. He pressed the gas pedal hard against the floor.

"I've wanted to do this my whole life!" he yelled.

Eighty . . . ninety . . . *one hundred miles per hour.* It was bumpy. Everything was vibrating. The plates in the little kitchen were rattling.

"Woo-*hoooooooooooo!*" Coke shouted. "Put the pedal to the metal, Dad! Burn rubber!"

"Slow down, Dad!" Pep said, gripping the armrests tightly.

"That's enough, Ben!" Mrs. McDonald shouted. "You proved your point. We *get* it! It goes fast!"

But it wasn't enough. The RV was still accelerating as the speedometer needle nosed past 110 miles per hour.

That's when Coke saw something in front of them. It was just a dot on the horizon at first; but as they got closer, it appeared to be a person. No, *two* people. They were waving their hands frantically.

"Somebody's out there, Dad!" Pep hollered, pointing.

"Hit the brakes!" ordered Mrs. McDonald.

"Steer around them!" shouted Coke.

Dr. McDonald took both suggestions, which sent the RV into a long skid and nearly caused it to flip over. Some of the cabinet doors flew open. Pots and pans came flying out and rattled against the floor.

The two people on the salt flat dove out of the way. The RV came within inches of mowing them down.

"That was *cool*, Dad!" Coke shouted when the RV had screeched to a halt. They all took a deep breath and then unfastened their seat belts and jumped out to see who was crazy enough to be running around in the middle of the Bonneville Salt Flats without a car.

The two people were lying on the ground. One was a man and the other was a woman. Their clothes were ripped and ragged.

It took a moment, but once the twins got a good

look at the faces, they realized they had seen these people before.

It was Bones and Mya!

"What are *you* doing out here?" Pep hollered.

"Water . . . water . . . ," they begged.

Bones and Mya could barely speak; their throats were too dry and sore. They were barely alive.

"Do you know these people?" Mrs. McDonald asked Pep.

"No!" Pep lied. "Of course not. Why would you think that?"

"Well, you just said 'What are *you* doing out here?'" Mrs. McDonald explained. "That sounds like you're talking to somebody you've met before."

"No, no, Mom," Coke explained. "She didn't say 'What are *you* doing out here?' She said 'What are you *doing* out here?' There's a big difference. It all depends on which word you emphasize, you see."

"I never met these people in my life," Pep lied.

She had to. She had been sworn to secrecy.

Dr. McDonald poured water over Bones's and Mya's faces. Mrs. McDonald helped them up and brought them into the RV, where it was shady and air-conditioned. Bones put a finger to his lips to let the twins know not to tell their parents who they were.

Mrs. McDonald made them some instant oatmeal.

After Dr. McDonald checked out the tires to make sure they weren't damaged by their little sprint, he tried to get Bones and Mya to explain why they were wandering around the Bonneville Salt Flats with no food or water. They pretended that it was too painful to speak and just pantomimed that they would be okay.

"We'll take you to the nearest gas station," Dr. McDonald finally said.

"Thank you," Mya croaked, looking up from the oatmeal.

In the back of the RV, Pep took out her notepad. She made a big question mark on it and handed it to Bones for him to write a reply.

SHE TRIED 2 KILL US

Who?

HIGGINS.

My health teacher??? She's alive?

YES. KIDNAPPED US. DROVE US OUT THERE. LEFT US 2 DIE.

U OK?

DON'T WORRY. MEET U AT BALL OF TWINE. GO THERE. <u>IMPORTANT!</u>

Dr. McDonald pulled into a gas station and insisted on giving twenty dollars to Bones and Mya before

they got out of the RV. They thanked him repeatedly and wrote down his address so they could repay the money when they could.

Go to Google Maps (http://maps.google .com/).

Click Get Directions.

In the A box, type Wendover UT.

In the B box, type Evanston WY.

Click Get Directions.

As the RV pulled away, Coke and Pep waved to Bones and Mya out the back window and wondered how they would ever get to Kansas.

After that morning excitement, the rest of the day seemed to go by in a blur. They passed the southern part of Great Salt Lake, which is the largest salt lake in the western hemisphere. It's three to five times as salty as the ocean. Just about anybody can float in it.

"Think it's possible to drown in there?" Pep wondered out loud.

"Sure," Coke replied. "If somebody holds your head under the water long enough."

Legend has it that there's a monster in Great Salt Lake with a body like a crocodile and a horse's head. Mrs. McDonald said she'd like to take a look and write about it for *Amazing but True*. But everyone agreed that they had enough salt for the day and decided to press on.

In Salt Lake City, behind the State Capitol, there is

what is called a "gravity hill." According to the locals, a guy named Emo was buried in the area. At midnight, his grave gives off a blue glow and his ghost warps gravity so that cars parked at the bottom of the gravity hill will roll uphill. Mrs. McDonald insisted they try it, but it didn't work. Maybe it does with a Mini Cooper or Smart Car, but not with an RV.

Then Mrs. McDonald wanted to drive three hours north of Salt Lake City to Blackfoot, Idaho—the Potato Capital of the World. They have the world's largest potato there (made of Styrofoam) and also the world's largest potato chip (about the size of a pizza). But the rest of the family voted against it, even if it meant they would not be able to sample the potato fudge or potato ice cream, which is sold in the gift shop.

It was still early in the day, so Dr. McDonald decided to see how many miles he could cover. A little over an hour from Salt Lake City, everybody whooped and hollered when they saw the sign that read . . .

Welcome to
Wyoming

"Did you know that Wyoming has the fewest people of any state?" Coke asked.

"Thank you, Mr. Know-It-All," his sister replied. "How much longer to the largest ball of twine in the world?"

"Seven hundred and eighty-five miles to Cawker City," replied Mrs. McDonald.

"Floor it, Dad!" Coke yelled. "Just like you did at the Bonneville Salt Flats."

"I don't think so," Dr. McDonald said. But he pushed the gas pedal down *just* a little harder, bumping the needle on the speedometer just past seventy miles per hour.

Everybody wanted to get to the largest ball of twine in Cawker City, Kansas, as quickly as possible for their own reasons. Coke and Pep wanted to get there because they had been assigned to stop an attack there. Mrs. McDonald wanted to get there to gather information for *Amazing but True*. And Dr. McDonald wanted to get there because, well, he could get it over with. Once he saw the stupid ball of twine, he reasoned, nobody

Go to Google Maps (http://maps.google.com/).

Click Get Directions.

In the A box, type Evanston WY.

In the B box, type Cheyenne WY.

Click Get Directions.

would ever ask him to go there again.

But first they had to get through Wyoming and a good part of Nebraska.

Dr. McDonald was tired from driving, but he refused to let Mrs. McDonald take over the wheel. Maybe it was sexist, but he felt that driving was his job. And besides, his wife was a terrible driver. One time she set out for a trip to San Diego and wound up in Fresno.

I-80 runs nearly four hundred miles across the bottom of Wyoming. Mrs. McDonald calculated that they could do it in less than six hours without stopping.

That would mean no side trip to Vernal, Utah, which calls itself the Dinosaur Capital of the World. Mrs. McDonald would not be able to buy petrified dino poop souvenirs in the gift shops there.

That would mean no side trip to Estes Park, Colorado, where the key to Hitler's bomb shelter is on display. Perfect *Amazing but True* material.

They would have to miss seeing the giant sculpture of Abraham Lincoln's head in Laramie, Wyoming.

They would have to skip Chimney Rock, a rock that doesn't even look like a chimney, anyway.

Halfway across the state, they passed a sign that read CONTINENTAL DIVIDE.

"Did you know that rivers west of this spot flow

into the Pacific Ocean?" Coke asked. "And rivers east of here empty into the Atlantic."

"Nobody cares, Smarty-Pants," Pep told him.

There was still a long way to go before they would see the largest ball of twine in the world. They would have to endure the spectacular forests, wildflowers, and roaring rivers of Wyoming. The bighorn sheep lumbering alongside the highway and the golden eagles circling overhead.

Eventually the Rockies flattened out and gave way to the Great Plains on the eastern part of the state. And finally, after four hundred miles and five and a half hours of driving across the largest rectangle in the world, they spotted a sign that read . . .

WELCOME TO NEBRASKA

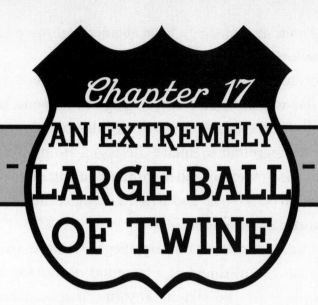

Chapter 17
AN EXTREMELY LARGE BALL OF TWINE

"I bet you guys can't name three things invented in Nebraska," Coke asked the family.

"No, but I'm sure you can," his sister replied.

"Kool-Aid, CliffsNotes, and Eskimo Pies!" Coke proclaimed.

"Ugh," Pep groaned.

"How can you possibly *know* that?" Mrs. McDonald asked.

"No clue," Coke replied. "Stuff just sticks in my head. I can't help it."

Mrs. McDonald took secret delight in the fact that Coke seemed to take after her. Maybe, she thought, after she retired from writing *Amazing but True*, Coke might take it over. They both seemed to have a love for useless information.

Dr. McDonald didn't even hear what Coke had said. He was so tired from driving at this point that he could barely stay awake. He decided not to search for a campground to spend the night. He pulled off I-80 at the first exit, headed for the first pair of golden arches he could find, and parked in the corner of the McDonald's lot.

He figured it was probably illegal to leave an RV overnight at a fast-food restaurant, but he did it, anyway. It's smarter to pay for a parking ticket than to fall asleep behind the wheel at seventy miles per hour.

The sleep did everyone good, and there was no ticket on the windshield in the morning. As a way of saying thank you, it was Egg McMuffins for everybody.

Mrs. McDonald took out her laptop and plotted the route to Cawker City, Kansas, home of the largest ball of twine in the world. It would be almost six hours of straight driving, she figured. When breakfast was

Go to Google Maps (http://maps.google.com/).

Click Get Directions.

In the A box, type Kimball NE.

In the B box, type Cawker City KS.

Click Get Directions.

done and the RV was gassed up, they were back on I-80.

"Any of you guys ever heard of Carhenge?" Mrs. McDonald asked, looking in her Nebraska guidebook.

"It's a replica of Stonehenge but with cars," Coke said, recalling a magazine article he'd seen while he and his mom were getting an oil change at Jiffy Lube. "Some guy half buried a bunch of old cars on his farm and welded them together to look like Stonehenge in England."

"How do you *remember* stuff like that?" Pep asked, incredulous.

"It's not that I remember so much," Coke replied. "It's that you remember so little."

"Where is this Carhenge?" Dr. McDonald asked.

"Two hours north and east of here," Mrs. McDonald replied, "in Alliance, Nebraska."

Dr. McDonald thought it over. They could stay on course and make it to the largest ball of twine in the world by late afternoon, *or* they could drive two hours out of their way to see a bunch of cars stuck in the dirt. It was a tough decision.

"Tell you what," he said. "Next summer we'll go to England, and I'll take you to the *real* Stonehenge."

"Deal!" everyone agreed.

They continued along I-80, passing the small towns

of Big Springs, Roscoe, and Paxton. They stopped for lunch in North Platte, home of the Fort Cody Trading Post, one of the largest souvenir shops in America. Standing outside was a gigantic Buffalo Bill, and inside there was a two-headed calf in a display case and a giant fiberglass buffalo. Anyone who can drive by *that* without stopping for a look has no sense of adventure.

It would be another 213 miles to Cawker City. But they were getting close now. Dr. McDonald pushed the gas pedal a little harder. The vast grasslands and treeless plains passing by made it seem as if the RV was moving in slow motion.

213

Near Elm Creek, Nebraska, Dr. McDonald pulled off the highway to head south on Route 183.

"Something tells me we're in Kansas," Coke said suddenly.

"What tells you?" asked Pep.

"*That* tells me!"

Then everybody saw the sign in the distance that read . . .

Welcome to
KANSAS

Hooting, hollering, and cheering erupted from the RV as they crossed the state line.

"Did you know that the state song of Kansas is 'Home on the Range'?" Coke announced.

"Big deal," Pep replied. "Ball of twine, here we come!"

The road was more narrow and gentler. Dr. McDonald eased off the gas to slow down and take in the scenery. They were in the country now, passing farms and churches, houses, and ball fields.

"This is the *real* America," Dr. McDonald said, glancing from side to side as he drove. "The America you don't see on TV."

Everyone was anxious to get to Cawker City, but they couldn't help but enjoy the view. It was so different from their home near San Francisco. Rolling hills. Endless fields of corn and wheat pastures. Grazing cows. Every few miles another small town. Phillipsburg . . . Kensington . . . Smith Center . . . Lebanon . . .

"Stop, Ben!" Mrs. McDonald suddenly yelled.

Dr. McDonald mashed on the brake, thinking he must have hit an animal or something. The RV screeched to a halt. At the side of the road there was a small chapel, a picnic table, and this . . .

Nearby was a stone marker announcing that this exact spot was the geographic middle of the continental United States, as determined by a government survey done around 1898.

They all got out of the RV to stretch their legs and check things out. An old man rode by on a wobbly bicycle.

"Excuse me," Mrs. McDonald asked the man. "Is this *really* the geographic center of the United States?"

"Yup," the man said without stopping.

"But that doesn't include Alaska and Hawaii, does it?" asked Coke.

"Nope."

"Does it account for the curvature of the earth?" asked Dr. McDonald.

"Don't rightly know," the man replied, and he continued pedaling on his way.

"Think of it," Mrs. McDonald said, snapping a photo of the marker. "We're standing at the exact midpoint of the continental United States."

"Great," Coke said. "Let's blow this pop stand."

So they did. Standing at the exact geographic center of the United States was, admittedly, interesting. But it was hard to get excited about it when they were so close to *the largest ball of twine in the world*.

When they got back on the road and saw a sign that said CAWKER CITY 25 MILES, they could almost taste it. The McDonalds had driven about 1,600 miles by this time. They had traveled more than halfway across the country. And finally they were within shouting distance of Cawker City.

"This had better be worth it," Dr. McDonald mumbled as they passed some cows grazing at the side of the road.

It wasn't long before they could see a water tower in the distance, and soon the words on it could be read—CAWKER CITY. The cornfields gave way to a cute little town. It was neighborhoody. A barbershop here, a luncheonette there. And then the big sign . . .

Welcome to
CAWKER CITY
Home of the World's Largest Ball of Twine

"*Woo-hoo!*" Coke hollered. "We made it!"

As they drove along Wisconsin Street into the

downtown area, they all leaned forward in their seats, each hoping to be the first to see the ball of twine. It shouldn't be hard to spot, they figured. Anything that is the largest of its kind in the world shouldn't be hard to spot.

Dr. McDonald found a parking space big enough for the RV, so he grabbed it. They could walk the rest of the way.

"Be careful," Pep warned her brother as they climbed out of the RV. "Something is gonna go down here. It's our job to stop it."

She took the backpack just in case she had to hit somebody with a yo-yo, or gouge their eyes out with her Pez dispenser.

The people of Cawker City aren't ashamed of living in the home of the largest ball of twine in the world. Just the opposite. They're proud of it. The sidewalks are painted with twine so visitors can take the Masterpiece Twine Walk to see paintings in storefront windows that have images of twine hidden in them. Kids compete to find them all.

Suddenly, almost without noticing, they came to a simple pavilion on the south side of the street.

And there it was.

Nearly nine tons of twine, rolled into a forty-foot ball.

You have to see it to believe it. The McDonalds just stopped and stared, openmouthed.

"Wow!" marveled Mrs. McDonald.

"It's so . . . big," Coke said.

"It's *amazing*," said Pep.

Even Dr. McDonald was impressed.

"That's an *extremely* large ball of twine," he said.

Mrs. McDonald got to work, snapping photos, taking notes, and interviewing tourists and locals for *Amazing but True*.

Why is there a giant twine ball in Cawker City, Kansas? Excellent question.

It turns out that in 1953 a farmer named Frank Stoeber started to roll spare pieces of twine in his barn. He never threw any away or reused it. He just kept rolling it into a ball, and the ball got bigger. After a few years, the ball was eight feet tall and weighed two and a half tons. By 1961, the year Stoeber donated the ball to Cawker City, it was eleven feet tall.

Stoeber passed away in 1974; but the people of Cawker City kept right on rolling twine, and the ball kept growing. In fact, every August they have a Twine-A-Thon, where anyone can pitch in and help. Today, the ball has almost 1,500 miles of twine on it.

"That's almost as far as we drove from home!" Pep marveled.

"They should make Frank Stoeber's story into a movie," Coke said, putting on his movie preview voice: *"In a world of isolation and despair, one dreamer from the heartland turned his twisted obsession into a tacky tourist destination and in the process bound his small hometown together and put it on the map. How did he do it? With twine."*

"Pretty inspiring, huh?" Coke asked.

Pep punched him and pulled him aside so she could talk without their parents hearing.

"Get serious!" she told him. "Do you even remember why we're here? There's going to be some kind of attack! And we've got to stop it."

The twins looked all around nervously. Every person in the immediate area was a suspect, but they were particularly on the lookout for odd-looking characters: guys in golf carts wearing bowler hats, evil health teachers, or anyone else who appeared to be out of the ordinary. So far nothing. Just a bunch of

normal-looking locals and tourists.

The twins were on the lookout for Bones and Mya, too, but they were nowhere to be seen.

Mrs. McDonald went into a little shop across the street and came out with—what else—two balls of twine.

"Your birthday is in three days," she said, handing one to each of them. "This is an early present."

"Gee thanks, Mom!" Coke said with fake enthusiasm. "It's just what I always wanted."

He stuffed the balls of twine in his backpack with the deck of cards, Frisbee, Pez dispenser, yo-yo, and assorted junk he had accumulated.

"Okay!" Dr. McDonald said, clapping his hands. "This was great, but we should get on the road and start heading for Washington. The wedding, you remember."

"No!" the twins protested. "We want to stay longer!"

"Why?" Dr. McDonald asked. "It's a giant ball of twine! You *saw* it."

Pep couldn't tell her dad about the imminent attack. She looked at her brother.

"We just want to take in the *enormity* of it, Dad,"

Coke explained. "I mean, this thing is humongous. We'll probably never be here again. It's not every day you get to see the largest ball of twine in the world, right?"

At that moment, a bicycle pulled up next to them. The rider was the old man they had seen earlier at the geographic center of the United States. He rolled to a stop.

"Pretty big, eh?" he said, gesturing toward the ball of twine.

"Oh yeah," Coke said. "Biggest in the world."

"Maybe," the old man said.

"I beg your pardon?" asked Mrs. McDonald.

"Ain't necessarily the biggest," the old man said.

"What?" asked Mrs. McDonald, perking up her ears. "Are you suggesting there's a *larger* ball of twine somewhere?"

"Could be."

"Where?" Mrs. McDonald demanded, almost desperately. "You've seen a bigger one?"

"In Minnesota," the old timer said. "Little town called Darwin. Never seen it myself. Some folks say it's bigger. Some folks say this one's bigger."

"You gotta be kidding me!" Coke exclaimed.

Pep suddenly realized why there was no attack in Cawker City. She knew why Bones and Mya hadn't

191

shown up. It was the *other* ball of twine that they were supposed to go to!

"Let's go!" she said. "We gotta get to Minnesota!"

"Yeah, let's go!" Coke exclaimed.

"Are you guys crazy?" Dr. McDonald shouted. "Minnesota is probably seven hours north of here! We have to get to Washington by July Fourth for Aunt Judy's wedding! I'm sure that other ball of twine looks just like this one, Bridge. I'm not driving—"

"Ben," Mrs. McDonald said, her hand on his shoulder. "I *must* see the other ball of twine!"

That was all she had to say. The three of them had to physically drag him back to the RV.

Chapter 18

SPAM
SPAM
SPAM
SPAM

A s they headed north on Route 81, Dr. McDonald was fuming. He was so angry, he couldn't speak. He did *not* want to go see another ball of twine.

In cartoons, animators typically have smoke pouring out of characters' ears to signal they're really mad. There might as well have been smoke pouring out of Dr. McDonald's ears.

But he was a devoted husband and father, too. Sometimes it seemed as

Go to Google Maps (http://maps.google.com/).

Click Get Directions.

In the A box, type Cawker City KS.

In the B box, type Lincoln NE.

Click Get Directions.

though he loved his family even more than he loved himself. And if his family wanted him to drive hours out of his way to Minnesota to see another @#$%^&* ball of twine, he decided, then, @#$%^&*, he would drive them there. That's the kind of a man he was.

Please excuse the language. This is just what was going through Dr. McDonald's mind.

He was so angry, in fact, that he had forgotten that the contents of the RV's holding tank had not been emptied since the family left California. It was nearly filled to the top now.

It crossed Coke's mind a few times that he should do a dump, but he never did anything about it. The thought of dropping four days' worth of human waste through a tube into a hole in the ground was not Coke's idea of a fun morning. He figured that when the time came that they *really* needed to do a dump, his father would let him know.

But Dr. McDonald wasn't talking. He didn't say a word to anybody for three hours. The sun was getting low in the sky, so as soon as he saw an RV CAMPING sign outside of Lincoln, Nebraska, he pulled off the highway.

And after a good night's sleep, at least *some* of his anger had subsided.

Driving up through Minnesota could be fun, he

tried to convince himself as they got back on I-80 toward Omaha.

He'd never been to Minnesota, he reasoned. It was always good to try new things.

Minnesota was supposed to be beautiful in the summer, he said silently.

Spontaneity makes for the best vacation memories, he decided.

It might even be *fun* to see another giant ball of twine, he thought.

But deep down inside, he didn't believe a word of it.

Go to Google Maps (http://maps.google.com/).

Click Get Directions.

In the A box, type Omaha NE.

In the B box, type Darwin MN.

Click Get Directions.

It's 440 miles from Omaha, Nebraska, to Darwin, Minnesota. Seven hours and twenty-five minutes of driving, if you don't stop. That's a lot of driving.

The RV was filled with tension. As they passed Omaha and crossed over into Iowa, Coke didn't even announce any useless information about the state. Mrs. McDonald pulled out an Iowa guidebook and began to leaf through it.

"Y'know, there's a forty-five ton concrete bull in Audubon," she said quietly. "It's the largest bull in the world. We should go see it. It's not far out of the way.

Its name is Albert."

"No!" Coke and Pep shouted from the back. "We want to get to the other ball of twine!"

"There's a ten-foot ear of corn in Coon Rapids," Mrs. McDonald announced a few minutes later. "And it rotates."

"No!" the kids barked. "We want to see the other ball of twine!"

"How about the Buddy Holly Monument in Clear Lake?" Mrs. McDonald suggested gently. "Buddy Holly sang 'Peggy Sue,' 'It's So Easy,' 'Rave On' . . ."

In the front seat, the grown-ups broke into an off-key version of "That'll Be the Day."

"No!" yelled the kids. "We want to see the other ball of twine!"

"How about the Hobo Museum?" Mrs. McDonald persisted. "It says here that while many people think of hobos as drunks and criminals, the Hobo Museum celebrates them as dignified men who preferred a relaxed lifestyle on the road without the pressures of owning homes and acquiring material possessions."

"I think I would like the life of a hobo," Dr. McDonald said. "No schedules or deadlines. No mortgage or phone bills. No office. You can dress the way you want, go where you want, and sleep when you want. And you get to see the world. Maybe I should become a hobo."

"How would we put the kids through college, dear?" asked Mrs. McDonald.

"Who needs college?" he replied. "The kids could become hobos too."

"No!" came shouts from the backseat. "Ball of twine!"

Mrs. McDonald continued to leaf through the guidebook but stopped suggesting interesting places to stop.

Dr. McDonald pulled off I-80 East at Des Moines and merged onto Interstate 35, which goes north-south and cuts Iowa almost perfectly in half. It seemed as if they had been driving forever. Heading north, it was another two hours before they crossed the state line.

There was no cheering from the backseat. No announcements about the Land of 10,000 Lakes. The

kids just wanted to get to the ball of twine in Darwin, which was another three hours away.

"Hit the brakes!" Mrs. McDonald suddenly shouted as they approached the exit for Interstate 90.

Dr. McDonald veered off to the shoulder of the road and screeched to a halt.

"What is it?" he said. "What's wrong?"

"The SPAM Museum," Mrs. McDonald announced. "I *must* go to the SPAM Museum."

"What?!" Dr. McDonald shouted. "You're kidding me! There's a museum devoted to SPAM?"

"No!" the kids shouted. "Ball of twine!"

"The SPAM Museum is less than a half an hour from here," Mrs. McDonald said calmly. "Take this exit, Ben."

"We really have to get to the ball of twine, Mom," Coke argued.

"No, we really have to get to the SPAM Museum," his mother replied sternly.

Dr. McDonald pulled off at the exit.

Yes, it's true. Austin, Minnesota, is the headquarters of Hormel, the company that makes SPAM. It probably never occurred to you, reader, that there would be a museum devoted to a gooey, spiced luncheon meat. But before opening this book, you'd probably never heard of the National Yo-Yo Museum or the Burlingame Museum of Pez Memorabilia either. It's a big country, and there's a lot of strange stuff in it.

The SPAM Museum is across the street from Hormel's meat plant. Yes, they have an entire building devoted to SPAM. Reluctantly, the kids got out of the RV and followed their mother inside. They were surprised that the admission was free.

"Of *course* it's free," Dr. McDonald told them. "The whole place is one big commercial for SPAM. They should pay *us* to come in here."

Dr. McDonald told the family that he had traumatic childhood memories of SPAM. His mother had forced him to eat it. He and his brother had called it "mystery meat."

The McDonalds were assigned to a tour group; and a tall, cheerful woman with a name tag that said JULIE introduced herself as their "SPAMbassador."

"Welcome to the SPAM Museum," she said. "How many of you enjoy SPAM?"

Some of the hands went up.

Julie told the group that seven *billion* cans of SPAM have been sold since it was introduced in 1937. The tour included just about everything you always

wanted to know about SPAM but were afraid to ask.

"I had no idea that lunch meat had such a fascinating history," Dr. McDonald said sarcastically as they entered the World War II exhibit.

"Oh yes," Julie the SPAMbassador said. "In fact, during the world war, a hundred million pounds of SPAM were sent to Allied soldiers."

"Did they eat it?" Coke said. "Or use it for ammunition?"

"They should have dropped a hundred million pounds of SPAM on Hitler," Dr. McDonald said. "Or they should have forced the Nazis to eat SPAM. They would have surrendered a lot sooner."

The McDonalds found it impossible to think about SPAM without giggling.

When the tour was over, Mrs. McDonald went to the gift shop. She picked up recipes for SPAMBURGERS and tried to decide whether she should buy a SPAM hat, necktie, flip-flops, or glow-in-the-dark SPAM boxer shorts for her husband. In the end, she decided to keep it simple. She bought a can of SPAM. In case of emergency, they could eat it. It didn't even have to be refrigerated. Coke and Pep wandered around the gift shop with their mom, snickering at all the SPAM-related products.

A man with a mustache, dressed like an old-time

policeman, was sitting by the door taking a snooze. He had a billy club in his hand.

"Check it out," Coke whispered, nudging his sister. "They have a guard in the SPAM Museum! Can you believe it? Do they actually think somebody would want to steal SPAM?"

"I don't think he's a real guard," Pep said. "He's a character, like at Disneyland."

"SPAM was invented in the 1930s," Mrs. McDonald pointed out. "I guess he's supposed to be a 1930s cop."

The mustachioed guard woke up with a snort.

"Say," he said, "would you kids like to try your hand at canning SPAM?"

"No thanks," Pep replied. "We really need to get back on the road."

"Come on, kids!" Mrs. McDonald said. "It will be fun! Sure, they'd love to can some SPAM."

"Follow me," the guard said.

He led Coke and Pep out the side door of the SPAM Museum and across the parking lot to the Hormel meat plant. The factory was closed for the day, but the smell of SPAM still hung in the air.

"This guard gives me the creeps," Pep whispered to her brother.

The twins followed the mustachioed guard into a huge room filled with canning equipment. All the

workers had gone home. In the middle of the room was a giant vat, about the size of a water tower. It was filled almost to the brim—with liquefied SPAM, of course.

"This is where we can the SPAM," the guard said.

"I figured that," Coke said.

"That's a *lot* of SPAM," Pep said.

"A hundred thousand gallons," the guard said. "Want to take a closer look?"

There was a narrow metal bridge that went about ten feet over to the top of the vat.

"We can see just fine from here," Pep replied.

"Don't you want to can a little SPAM?" the guard asked. "Bring it back home as a souvenir?"

"I'd really like to," Coke replied, "but I need to get back, y'know, and poke my eyes with hot needles."

"You should *really* take a closer look." The guard had pulled his billy club out of its holster and was rapping it against the palm of his left hand. He had a familiar smile on his face.

"You're not a real guard, are you?" Pep asked.

"No, I'm not."

With that, the guard reached behind one of the machines and put on a bowler hat.

"It's the bowler dude!" Coke shouted. "Run!"

"Not so fast!" the bowler dude said. He grabbed

both of them from behind and jammed the billy club hard against their necks.

"That wasn't very nice what you did to my brother," he said, pulling them toward the giant vat of SPAM.

"Your brother?" Pep asked, trying to get the club away from her windpipe. "Who's your brother?"

"The guy at Sand Mountain?" Coke asked. "You two are brothers?"

"My brother has a nasty bump on the back of his head, thanks to you kids," the bowler dude said, tightening his grip on the club.

"Your brother threw us in a pit up there!" Coke said, struggling to break free. "He was going to leave us there to die! And you were the guys who were chasing us to the edge of the cliff in golf carts. You've been trying to kill us!"

"And it's too bad we failed earlier," the bowler dude said, breathing heavily on their necks, "because now I'll have to do it myself."

"What are you going to *do* to us?" Pep whimpered. She was crying now.

"SPAM, SPAM, SPAM, SPAM." The bowler dude started singing the song made famous in the old *Monty Python's Flying Circus* TV show. He had an evil smile on his face.

"No!" Pep shouted.

"Get in the vat!" the bowler dude instructed.

"It's disgusting!" Pep shouted.

"I said, get *in*!" the bowler dude insisted. "And don't try anything funny, like you did with my brother."

"Hit him, Coke!" Pep yelled. "You know karate! Kick him! Do something!"

But Coke was powerless. When he was taught how to punch and kick in karate, the opponents just stood there and held up soft pads to absorb the blows. They never fought back. This guy had a billy club pressed against his throat. If he tried any of the karate moves he had learned, his windpipe would be crushed in a second.

Pep, on the other hand, had no reservations. She had never taken a self-defense course, but she knew there was one spot on the body where every male is vulnerable to a good, swift kick. The bowler dude had her from behind, but she bent her knee quickly and rammed her foot backward into his groin.

"Ugg!" the bowler dude groaned.

Pep wasn't finished. Summoning up a previously unused source of fury, she started kicking, punching, and spitting in the bowler dude's face. He tried to hit her with the club; but he was in so much pain that he fell backward, pulling Coke and Pep with him. The three of them toppled over; and the next thing any of them knew, they had fallen into the vat of SPAM.

Pep *still* wasn't finished. She scooped up a handful of the stuff and slapped it against the bowler dude's eyes, blinding him, at least temporarily. Then she pushed his head down with both of her hands until it was below the surface of the liquefied SPAM.

Coke could only watch, shocked, as he grabbed the edge of the vat to prevent himself from slipping below the surface himself. He had never seen his sister show aggression before.

"That's enough!" he yelled at her. "You'll kill him!"

"He tried to kill *us*!" Pep yelled back as she held the bowler dude's head under. "It's self-defense!"

"Let's just get out of here!" Coke said.

He pulled himself up and out of the vat, then reached down a hand to help his sister up onto the metal walkway. The bowler dude's head was still covered by the SPAM. It wasn't clear if he was dead or alive.

"Do you think he'll be . . . ground up and put in cans of SPAM?" Pep asked as they ran out of the room.

"Who would know?" Coke replied.

They ran across the parking lot, trying their best to wipe off as much SPAM as possible. But it was useless. They were covered from head to toe.

"Where did you learn how to do all that self-defense stuff?" Coke asked Pep just before they reached the RV.

"Something just came over me," she replied. "I was fighting for my life."

Their parents must have heard them approaching, because they rushed out of the RV to greet the twins, stopping short of any hugs.

"Where *were* you two?" Mrs. McDonald said. "Is that SPAM?"

"What happened?" Dr. McDonald said. "I had no idea that canning SPAM was so messy."

"You have no idea, Dad," Coke said. "Let's get out of here."

By the time the twins changed their clothes and the family got on the road, it was already dark. They were still almost three hours from Darwin. Everybody was exhausted. The twins tried to forget what had happened in the canning room. Mrs. McDonald looked in the guidebook and found a campground near Owatonna off Interstate 35 North along the way to Minneapolis. Not too far.

They hadn't made it all the way to the Darwin ball of twine, but they were close. It would be a two-and-a-half-hour drive in the morning.

"You should really do a dump," Dr. McDonald told

Coke as they pulled into their campsite.

"Can I do it in the morning, Dad?" he asked. "It's really late."

"Okay, but let's use the regular bathroom here," Dr. McDonald instructed the family. "Our holding tank is probably full."

Coke gathered his toiletry bag and found the nearest bathroom, a little outhouse not far from their RV. He opened the door, looked in the mirror, and saw this written on it in lipstick:

6362562558638936893438484346346489766684346873668437625
22333321222112213333121223232313333112223242321223332

At first, he thought it was just a bunch of random numbers or a prank played by some kids. But then he realized it was something else. It was another cipher.

"You gotta be kidding me!" he said out loud.

Quickly, he memorized the order of the numbers and then smudged the mirror to obliterate the message.

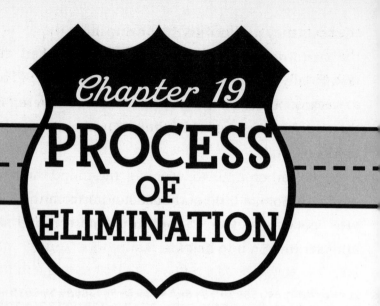

Chapter 19
PROCESS
OF
ELIMINATION

As soon as Coke got back to the RV, he wrote out the new cipher for his sister.

66362562558638936893434384843463464897666684346873668437625
32233333212221122133331212232332313333112223242321223332

"Numbers?" she asked. "Now we've got to figure out *numbers*?"

"*You're* the queen of the ciphers," he replied. "I'm sure you'll figure it out."

Pep looked at the cipher for a few minutes. It was incomprehensible. The only pattern she could recognize was that the top row had higher numbers than the bottom row. Whoever was tormenting them with these ciphers was making each one harder than the last. Finally, she decided the best thing to do would be to sleep on it. Maybe the answer would come to her in the middle of the night like the last time.

It didn't.

Breakfast was cold cereal eaten out of cardboard bowls with plastic spoons. Nothing fancy. Everybody was anxious to get up to Darwin, Minnesota, and see the largest—or maybe second largest—ball of twine in the world. As they were getting ready to leave the campground, Mrs. McDonald suggested they all go out to the movies that evening. She had checked the internet and seen that there was a theater in Litchfield, just a few miles from Darwin.

Dr. McDonald pulled the RV onto Interstate 35 heading north toward Minneapolis. They had only driven a few miles down the road when he snapped his fingers.

"We forgot to do a dump back at the campground!" he exclaimed. "The holding tank is filled to the brim!"

Go to Google Maps (http://maps.google.com/).

Click Get Directions.

In the A box, type Owatonna MN.

In the B box, type Darwin MN.

Click Get Directions.

"I'll do it today, Dad," Coke said. "I promise."

"You'd better!"

To get to Darwin, you drive up I-35, and before you get to Minneapolis, you jump on I-494 briefly and then west on the smaller Route 12. From there, it's about an hour—a straight shot into Darwin.

The town looked a little like Cawker City, Kansas, where the *other* giant ball of twine was located. Small-town America. Driving down the main street, they started to see signs: THE TWINE BALL INN. TWINE BALL ANTIQUE SHOP. SOUVENIR TWINE BALLS SOLD HERE. Dr. McDonald made a left onto First Street. He drove by a park and a water tower, and then they saw a large gazebo covered by Plexiglas panels.

"Thar she blows!" Coke yelled.

Dr. McDonald went a block farther, turned the corner, and parked the RV on a side street.

"Be careful now," Coke whispered to his sister as he grabbed their backpacks. "Something's gonna happen here for sure. Something bad. We've got to stop it. Keep your eyes open."

"But we don't know *when*," Pep whispered back. "It may not even be today."

They walked around the corner and joined the group of people mingling around the ball of twine. It was, of course, enormous—just about filling the gazebo.

"Behold," Mrs. McDonald said. "The largest ball of twine in the world!"

But once you've seen one gigantic ball of twine, you've pretty much seen 'em all. It was still interesting to look at, but some of the novelty had worn off.

"It looks pretty much like the other one," noted Dr. McDonald. "I can't believe we drove so far out of our way to see this."

"I think this one is a little bigger than the one in Kansas," Pep said. "It was definitely worth the trip."

"Think of it this way, Dad," Coke said. "Now we've seen the *two* biggest balls of twine in the world! How many people can say that?"

Dr. McDonald shook his head sadly and went to sit on a bench nearby to read a book. He had seen enough giant balls of twine to last a lifetime.

Mrs. McDonald seemed to be just as fascinated with the Darwin twine ball as she had been with the one in Cawker City. She insisted on reading every pamphlet and the wall plaque about the ball's history.

Apparently, a few years before Frank Stoeber started rolling his ball of twine in Kansas, a farmer named Francis A. Johnson began rolling one in Darwin. Johnson even used a crane so he could lift the ball to continue rolling it properly.

For years, the two men had a sort of long-distance dueling-twine-ball race going as their respective balls got bigger and bigger.

After Frank Stoeber died in 1974, you would have thought Francis Johnson would have claimed victory and retired. But he kept right on going, rolling twine four hours a day, every day, until he died in 1989. By that time, his twine ball was 17,900 pounds and thirteen feet in diameter.

Mrs. McDonald went across the street to interview some locals about the twine ball. Coke and Pep walked among the crowd looking for suspicious characters.

Most of the people standing around looked fairly normal, but one couple caught their eyes. With clunky cameras around their necks and Minnesota guidebooks in their hands, they were obviously tourists. The man had a bushy mustache and the woman had on round, oversized sunglasses. They spoke in loud German accents.

"Vee have a ball of twine in Düsseldorf much bigger zan zees vun," the man said to nobody in particular.

"Oh yes," said the woman. "Our twine ball makes zees vun look like a little marble."

A few of the locals shot glares at the German couple, but nobody argued with them. Minnesotans are known for their politeness. Coke and Pep sidled over to the couple so they could hear better.

"Our German twine ball is so large zat it exerts its own gravitational force," boasted the man. "It influences zuh ocean tides, you know."

"Yes," the woman agreed. "Zare is some concern zat zuh gravitational pull of our twine ball might cause zuh moon to crash into Earth."

The German couple looked directly at Coke and Pep as they spoke. And then the woman took off her sunglasses and the man pulled off his mustache.

"Bones!" Coke said.

"Mya!" Pep said, a little too loud.

"Shhhhh!" Mya said, putting the sunglasses back on. "We're looking to prevent an attack. We've been here for two days. We're exhausted."

"How did you *get* here?" Pep asked. "The last time we saw you, it was at the Bonneville Salt Flats. You guys were almost dead!"

"It's a long story," Mya said. "The important thing is that we're here and the twine ball is safe. So far, anyway."

"Have you seen anything suspicious?" Coke asked.

"No," said Bones. "But we intercepted another text message that said somebody's gonna try something here any day. So we can't let down our guard for a second."

"Why don't you take a break?" Pep said. "We'll relieve you for a while."

Bones and Mya looked at each other as if they weren't sure the twins could be trusted to handle whatever might happen in their absence. But they *were* tired, and the idea of taking a break sounded good.

"That would be wonderful," Bones said. "We'll meet you back here in an hour."

"Auf Wiedersehen," Mya said.

"Do you think those two are boyfriend and girlfriend?" Pep asked her brother after Bones and Mya walked away.

"How should I know?" Coke asked, irritated. He always found gossip to be annoying.

They walked around the twine ball for a long time, pretending to look interested. In fact, they were looking at the people who really *were* interested. And then, suddenly, Coke stopped and tugged at his sister's sleeve.

"Hey, you see that lady over there?" he whispered. "Does she look familiar to you?"

Pep looked at the tall woman on the other side of the twine ball. The scarf over her head made it hard to tell what her face looked like.

The woman was taking pictures of the ball like all the other tourists. But then, for a moment, she reached out and pressed her hand against the ball.

She was wearing white gloves.

"It's Mrs. Higgins!" Pep exclaimed. "Our health teacher!"

"Shhhhhhh!" Coke clapped a hand over his sister's mouth. "Be cool."

"What's Mrs. Higgins doing here?" Pep whispered. "Do you think it's a coincidence?"

"Gee, I don't know," Coke said. "Do you think it was a coincidence that the school burned down right after she locked us in the detention room?"

"Maybe she's going to try to kill us again," Pep said.

"I don't think so," Coke replied. "She doesn't even seem to realize we're here."

At that moment, Mrs. Higgins took one last look at the ball of twine and walked out of the gazebo.

"Where's she going?" Pep asked.

"I don't know," Coke replied, grabbing his sister's hand, "but wherever it is, that's where we're going. Come on!"

Pep took out her cell phone and sent a quick text to her mother.

> We went 2 look 4 souvenirs

Mrs. Higgins crossed the street, turned the corner, and walked briskly down the same street where the RV was parked. Coke and Pep followed, ducking behind cars and bushes so they would not be seen.

Mrs. Higgins walked right past the RV and got into a red convertible parked three spaces in front of it. The car started.

"She's leaving!" Pep whispered.

"Get in the RV!" Coke barked.

"Why?"

"Just get in!"

The RV door, as usual, was unlocked, and the key in the ignition. The twins climbed into the front seats. Coke turned the key.

"What are you doing?" his sister shouted. "You're

not old enough to drive!"

"Sez who?" Coke asked. "Look! She's getting away! Fasten your seat belt!"

He put the RV into gear and pulled out of the parking space.

"Are you crazy?" Pep yelled. "You don't know how to drive this thing! What if you damage the RV?"

"It's okay," Coke told her as he put his foot on the gas. "It's a rental."

The red convertible made a left at the corner and drove slowly down the street. Coke followed, keeping a respectable distance between them.

"Mom and Dad are going to *freak*!" Pep complained.

"Relax, they'll never find out," Coke said. "Look, we know that Mrs. Higgins is an assassin. We've got to find out where she's going."

The red convertible drove a few blocks and then turned down a short, steep hill and into the parking lot of a pizza place at the end of a strip mall. There were only two other cars in the lot, and Coke didn't want to attract attention by joining them. Instead, he stopped at the top of the hill and drove near a guardrail that overlooked the parking lot.

"Where did she go?" Pep asked as she scanned the lot.

They got out of the RV to look around. When they

glanced down, they could see the red convertible parked directly below.

"Shhhhh," Coke said.

The twins watched as Mrs. Higgins took off her seat belt and removed her gloves. She opened the driver's side door and got out of the convertible. Then she opened the trunk and took something out of it. It looked like a plastic container of some sort with straps on each side. She went around to the front of the convertible and began to tie the straps to the bumper.

"What's she doing?" Pep whispered.

"I don't know," Coke replied. "Why would somebody strap something to the bumper of their car?"

Mrs. Higgins went back to the trunk again and took out a smaller container with a lid on it. She removed the lid and went to the front of the car. Her body was blocking their line of sight, so the twins couldn't tell if it was a liquid, a powder, or what it was that she was pouring into the larger container that was strapped to the front bumper. But she was leaning over the container, definitely pouring something into it.

"I think it's some kind of bomb!" Pep whispered.

"She's gonna drive it into the ball of twine and blow it up!" Coke whispered.

"Why would she do a crazy thing like that?"

"Maybe she's a suicide bomber!"

"But why would a suicide bomber bother blowing up a ball of twine?" Pep asked.

"Don't you see?" Coke told his sister. "The largest ball of twine is a symbol of America, just like the Liberty Bell or the White House. No other country in the world would produce a dreamer who spends thirty years of his life rolling a giant ball of twine. It's symbolic of the American spirit: hard work, determination, creativity, freedom, and all that stuff."

"If she was going to destroy a symbol of America," Pep asked, "why wouldn't she drive a car into the Liberty Bell or the White House?"

"Because she *can't*!" Coke told his sister. "They've got armed guards there 24/7. If she made one false move toward the Liberty Bell, the security people would take her down in a second."

"Maybe you're right," Pep whispered. "There's no security around here. It probably never even occurred to the police that somebody would try to harm the ball of twine. It's the perfect target!"

Mrs. Higgins put the cap on the container that was strapped to the front bumper of her convertible. She got back into the car and lit a cigarette. It looked as if her hands were shaking.

"She's preparing mentally," Coke whispered. "She's

working up the nerve. Then she's gonna ram the car into the ball of twine and blow it to kingdom come. She'll be dead, but she will have struck a blow against America. And the attack will be on the evening news all over the world tomorrow."

"We need to call the cops," Pep said, taking out her cell phone.

"No time for that," Coke told her. "We gotta do something, and fast."

"What are we gonna do?" Pep asked, looking in the backpack. "Throw a Frisbee at her? Attack her with a yo-yo?"

Mrs. Higgins flicked an ash from her cigarette out of the convertible. Coke thought it over. And then he brightened.

"I got it," he finally said.

"Got what?"

"Shhhhh! Follow me."

Coke got out and tiptoed over to the side of the RV. He opened a panel on the side, took out a pair of yellow rubber gloves, and put them on.

"What are you doing?" Pep whispered.

"It's time to do a dump," Coke replied as he uncurled the thick hose and attached it to the connectors under the RV.

"Wait a minute," his sister said. "You mean to say

you're going to drop the contents of our toilet on Mrs. Higgins?"

Coke just grinned and nodded his head.

"That's disgusting!" she said.

"I know!" he replied. "That's why I'm doing it. She's in for a big surprise."

Coke gave the connector one last turn until the hose clicked into place. Then he took the other end of the hose and pulled it toward the guardrail. It reached just long enough to hang over the ledge and dangle above the convertible.

Down below, Mrs. Higgins took one last puff of her cigarette and flicked it away. Then she took some hand sanitizer out of the glove compartment and wiped off the steering wheel. Finally, she pulled the gloves back on.

"She's getting ready to leave!" Pep said. "She's putting her seat belt on!"

"Perfect!" Coke said. "That will make it harder for her to get out of the car. Quick! Go pull the lever next to the hose."

At the same moment that Mrs. Higgins reached for her key to start her car, Pep pulled the lever next to the hose.

And that's when five days' worth of human waste slid down out of the holding tank, through the hose,

and dropped into the driver's seat of the red convertible parked directly below.

If you sat down and made a list of the most disgusting things that could possibly happen to a human being, having almost a week's worth of human waste—both liquid and solid—fall on your head would probably be right up there at the top.

Mrs. Higgins let out a momentary shriek when the first few ounces hit her head but then wisely decided to close her mouth. She tried to unhook her seat belt, but by that time everything was wet and slippery.

The hose was thick, maybe five inches in diameter. It didn't take long for the front seat of the convertible to be covered. Mrs. Higgins thrashed around helplessly, like a fish on the floor of a rowboat.

"Let's blow this pop stand!" Coke said gleefully.

The twins scrambled to detach the hose from the connector and put it back in place. They took one last look over the railing to see Mrs. Higgins still sitting there, helpless and weeping, in a pool of human waste up to her neck. The twins jumped back into the RV. Coke started it, jammed it into reverse, and peeled out of there.

As they drove back into town, Coke and Pep were screaming and hooting and high-fiving each other as if they had just won the Super Bowl.

"It'll take her a long time to clean *that* off!" Coke hollered.

"She won't be driving that car into *anything* for a while," Pep yelled.

"You know what they say," Coke told his sister. "When all you've got are lemons, make lemonade."

"And those weren't lemons!" his sister shrieked.

They drove back to the center of Darwin, laughing all the way. Luckily, the parking space where the RV had been was still open. Not so luckily, there were two people standing in it.

Their parents.

"You two are *so* grounded!" Mrs. McDonald hollered.

Chapter 20

GROUNDED

The twins had done a lot of foolish things in their lives to make their parents angry. There was the time they jumped off a trampoline with umbrellas. The time they dialed 911 to see how long it would take for the cops to show up. The time they thought it would be fun to roll down the hill near the mall in shopping carts. Coke wound up in the emergency room after that one.

But they had never done anything as foolish, dangerous, and yes, let's say it—stupid—as going on a joyride in a recreational vehicle.

"Are you kids out of your *minds*?" Mrs. McDonald shouted when Coke pulled the RV back into the parking spot. "Do you have one brain between the two of you? What were you thinking? We could all be in jail right now! You said you were going to look for souvenirs! Where were you? We thought the RV had been stolen!"

Veins were sticking out of Mrs. McDonald's neck. People were starting to stare. It was causing a scene on the street.

"Oh, don't worry," Dr. McDonald assured the gathering crowd. "This isn't child abuse, folks. My kids just went out for a little ride . . . *in our rented RV*! They turn thirteen years old the day after tomorrow. I guess they think they're old enough to drive now."

"Can't blame you for screaming at 'em, pal," a guy walking by said. "If they were my kids, I'd ship 'em off to military school."

"We're really sorry, Dad," Pep said sincerely as she scampered into the backseat where she belonged. "We'll never do it again."

"Why did you do it *this* time?" asked her mother. "Do you have an explanation? I'd like to hear it."

Pep looked at her brother, who was slinking out of the driver's seat.

"Uh, we went to do a dump," Coke said. It was the truth, technically.

"You went to do a *dump*!?" Dr. McDonald was incredulous.

"That was the job you gave me," Coke reminded him. "The holding tank was really full, Dad. I promised I would do a dump today, and I felt bad that I forgot to do it yesterday. I always keep my promises, y'know."

Dr. McDonald was too upset to speak. He slapped his forehead and walked around in a circle on the sidewalk trying to regain his composure.

"Who said you could drive?" asked Mrs. McDonald.

"You're always telling us that we should take the initiative," Coke said lamely.

"You're *minors*!" Dr. McDonald said, exploding. "It's against the law for you to drive a motor vehicle! You could have been arrested! Mom and I could have been arrested! The police would say we're neglecting our kids! Did you ever think of *that*?"

"Calm down, Dad," Coke said. "You'll give yourself a coronary. Everything's fine. We did the dump. The RV doesn't have a scratch on it, and nobody got hurt. So what's the big deal?"

Dr. McDonald climbed into the driver's seat mumbling "It's a *rental*!" and how this sort of thing never happened when *he* was a kid. He drove out of Darwin aggressively, stomping on the gas pedal at every green light and stomping on the brake when the lights turned red. It was the only way he could express his anger.

They drove in silence for several miles until Coke worked up the courage to speak.

"May I ask one question, Dad?"

"What is it?" Dr. McDonald said sharply.

"When we're at home and you ground us, we have to stay in the house. I understand that. But how do you ground us when we're in an RV?"

Pep rolled her eyes. Sometimes, she wished, her brother should just keep his mouth shut.

"I'll tell you how," Dr. McDonald replied. "Your mother and I are going out to a nice dinner and a movie tonight . . . *alone*. You two are going to stay at the campground and think about what you did."

"Fair enough," Coke said sheepishly.

I don't know if you've ever stayed at an RV campground. Some of them are fully equipped with game rooms, stores, Ping-Pong tables, swimming pools, basketball courts, WiFi, and videos. Others just have an electrical hookup for your RV, a septic tank (so you can do a dump), and pretty much nothing else.

Mrs. McDonald purposely found a campground for the night that had *no* amenities. The place was basically a big parking lot with an office. After he checked

in, Dr. McDonald told the twins to get out of the RV.

"We'll be at the movies," he said. "See if you can make it through the next few hours without getting into trouble."

With that, Dr. and Mrs. McDonald drove away.

"What do you wanna do?" Pep asked.

"I don't know. What do *you* wanna do?" her brother replied.

"I asked you first."

There wasn't a whole lot to do. The twins put their backpacks on the nearest picnic table. Coke took out the Frisbee and flipped it casually to his sister. Then he ran about ten yards out into the parking lot.

"Do you think what we did was wrong?" Pep asked as she flipped the Frisbee back to him.

"Mrs. Higgins tried to kill us!" Coke said. "All we did was do a dump on her head."

"No," Pep said, catching his return throw. "I mean, was it wrong to drive the RV?"

"Oh," Coke replied. "Well, yeah, *that* was wrong. But it was right to do the dump on Mrs. Higgins's head, because it prevented her from blowing up the ball of twine. And how could we do the dump on her head and prevent her from blowing up the ball of twine if we didn't drive the RV? The right we did compensated for the wrong we did. So, all in all, I say we did the right thing."

Pep couldn't argue with his logic.

"It was fun, wasn't it?" Coke asked. "Doing the dump, I mean."

"Yeah." She giggled.

They threw the Frisbee back and forth a number of times, and Coke had to admit that his sister was getting better. She had learned to hold the Frisbee level as she released it. She didn't throw it very hard, but she was throwing it accurately. He hardly ever had to go chase it down.

When they got tired of playing Frisbee, they opened their backpacks looking for something else to do. Pez dispensers, yo-yos, balls of twine, and the deck of cards were scattered across the picnic table. Pep pulled out her pad and suddenly remembered the most recent cipher they had received. In all the excitement, she had completely forgotten about it.

6362562558638936893438484346346489766684346873668437625
4223333321222112213333121223233231333311222324232122332

Together they sat down at the picnic table and examined the cipher closely.

"The numbers in the first row are all higher than the numbers in the second row," Coke said.

"Brilliant, Einstein," his sister replied. "Did you notice that the numbers in the bottom row are all *1*, *2*, or *3*, except for a single *4*?"

"The numbers must correspond to letters in some way," Coke said. "It can't be as simple as *1* means *A*, *2* means *B*, and so on, because the bottom row would be almost all the same three letters."

"I can see some patterns," Pep pointed out. "In the top row, *8 4 3* is repeated three times. And in the bottom row, *1 2 2* is repeated three times. And look, the repeating digits are in the same place—on top of each other. That's got to mean something."

"The top and bottom rows are related to each other in some way," Coke guessed. "Maybe the code is *6 3*, *6 2*, *3 2*, and so on."

At that point, Coke's cell phone beeped. A text had come in from his father.

U KIDS OK? WERE SORRY WE GOT SO MAD

Coke texted back

no prob.

"Hey!" Pep said suddenly. "Let me see your phone for a sec."

"Why?"

"Just let me see it."

He handed his sister the cell, and she peered at the keypad. Slowly, her eyes widened and a smile spread across her face.

"Look!" she said excitedly. "There are no *1*s on the top line of the cipher!"

"So?"

"Just like the number *1* on the telephone keypad has no letters that go with it!"

"I don't read you," Coke said, confused.

"Don't you see?" Pep said. "Number *2* on the telephone keypad represents the letters *A*, *B*, and *C*. Number *3* represents *D*, *E*, and *F*. Number *4* represents *G*, *H*, and *I*. And so on. Each number on the keypad stands for three letters."

"But that doesn't help us," Coke said, "because every number in the cipher can be any of three different letters."

"That's right. It's the *bottom* row that tells us which letter it is!" Pep said excitedly. "See? The first column of numbers is *6* and *3*. The *6* on the keypad represents the letters *M*, *N*, and *O*. And the *3* tells us it's the *third* letter. So the message begins with the letter *O*!"

"Well, if *6* and *3* equals the letter *O*," Coke said, "then the next letter in the message is represented by

6 and *2*. And that would be . . ."

They looked at the keypad and said it together: "*N*."

The next number was a *3*, with a *2* underneath it. They looked at the keypad and saw that the *3* could be *D*, *E*, or *F*; and the *2* meant it was the second of those, the letter *E*.

"*O-N-E*," Pep said as she wrote it down on her pad. "That's probably the first word of the message!"

The twins quickly figured out that every time there was a *6* on the top row and a *3* beneath it, that represented the letter *O*. And every time there was a *4* on the top row and a *3* beneath it, that represented the letter *I*. Every time there was an *8* on the top row and a *1* beneath it, that represented the letter *T*. They rushed to fill in the rest of the letters.

625625 meant *oclock*.

5863 meant *June*.

893689 meant *twenty*.

34384 meant *fifth*.

"The infinity room!" Coke said excitedly. "*8 4 3 4 6 3 4 6 4 8 9 7 6 6 6* means *the infinity room*."

"And *8 4 3 4 6 8 7 3 6 6 8 4 3 7 6 2 5* means . . ." Pep said as she worked it out, "*the house on the rock!*"

They repeated the message out loud together.

"ONE OCLOCK JUNE TWENTY FIFTH THE INFINITY ROOM THE HOUSE ON THE ROCK."

Chapter 21
A WRONG TURN

Now the twins were furious. *The house on the rock!* Coke ripped the sheet of paper out of the pad, crumpled it up into a ball, and tossed it in the trash can next to the picnic table.

"What is this with a house on a rock?" he sputtered. "If they want us to go to this stupid house so badly, why don't they tell us where it is? Oh no, that would make too much sense!"

"And today is June twenty-third," Pep said, checking the date on the cell phone. "We only have two days to get there."

The sound of wheels on gravel made the twins look up and see the family's RV pulling into the parking lot. It was hard to believe three hours had gone by. Pep slipped her pad back into her backpack so her parents wouldn't see it.

"What have you kids been doing?" Dr. McDonald said cheerfully as he hopped out of the driver's seat. The movie must have been a comedy, the twins figured. Any anger their parents felt before they left was gone.

"Nothing exciting," Coke replied. "Played Frisbee mostly."

Their parents sat down at the picnic table with leftovers they had brought back from dinner, and gave the food to the kids. They said they had done some thinking about the rest of the trip. Aunt Judy's wedding would be in Washington on July Fourth, so they had eleven days to drive 1,167 miles. Mrs. McDonald felt there was plenty of time to stop off at interesting spots along the way and gather information for *Amazing but True*. She pulled a Minnesota guidebook out of her purse.

They were an hour and a half from Minneapolis, she told them. With that as a starting point, they could check out the Mall of America. It was one of the biggest malls in the world, and it was right nearby. In Belle Plaine, there was a two-story outhouse that attracts a lot of tourists. But that would be an hour out of the way, a long way to go to see a toilet.

In Rothsay, Minnesota, there was a nine-thousand-pound statue of a chicken. And in Frazee, there was the world's largest turkey.

In a town called Virginia, they had a giant floating statue of the Minnesota state bird: the loon. But it was more than three hours north. And the Sandpaper Museum, in Two Harbors, Minnesota, was almost as far. Even Mrs. McDonald had second thoughts about driving three hours to look at sandpaper. If they were going to go that far north, they might as well drive a little farther to Hibbing, which was the home of the world's largest open pit iron ore mine and also the boyhood home of Bob Dylan.

"I could spend a month just in Minnesota," Mrs. McDonald said wistfully.

"No wonder the state bird is a loon," Coke remarked.

"Anything in your guidebook about houses on rocks?" Coke asked.

"No," his mother replied. "Why?"

"Just wondering."

There was no way for the twins to find where the mysterious house on the rock was located. They would just have to wait and hope they received another cipher. In the end, Mrs. McDonald decided to visit just one location in Minneapolis: the Museum of

Questionable Medical Devices.

Mrs. McDonald read out loud from her guidebook and described this amazing museum that collected two hundred fifty weird contraptions that supposedly used electricity, radio waves, magnets, or vibrations to cure everything from arthritis to acne. A century ago, apparently, bogus scientists spent a lot of time dreaming up fraudulent devices such as the Bio-Electric Shield, the Dynameter, and Boyd's Battery, which hung around the neck to ward off the earth's magnetic rays. The Rejuvenator reversed the aging process. The Spectro-Chrome used six colored lights to cure six different diseases if you sat in front of it with no clothes on. The Psychograph was a bowl-shaped sensor that you put on your head to measure the bumps to determine your personality traits.

"Anybody who used one of those things should have his head examined," Coke remarked.

The next morning, June twenty-fourth, the McDonalds headed for St. Paul. The address for The Museum of Questionable Medical Devices, interestingly, turned out to be the same as for the

Go to Google Maps (http://maps.google.com/).

Click Get Directions.

In the A box, type Darwin MN.

In the B box, type Minneapolis MN.

Click Get Directions.

Science Museum of Minnesota.

"Excuse me," Mrs. McDonald asked a lady at the information desk, "where is The Museum of Questionable Medical Devices?"

"I'm very sorry," the lady replied, "but that museum is closed."

"Well, when does it open?"

"Uh, never," the lady said. "It closed a few years ago."

"What do you mean it's *closed*?" Mrs. McDonald put her hands on her hips, and her voice rose.

"Calm down, Bridge," Dr. McDonald said.

"I'm very sorry," the lady behind the desk said. "But that museum no longer exists."

"Do you know who I am?" Mrs. McDonald shouted. "I run a very popular website called *Amazing but True*. Maybe you've heard of it?"

"Mom," Pep said.

"No, I haven't heard of your website," the lady said, looking around for a guard. "I'm sorry, ma'am."

"My family and I drove all the way from California!" Mrs. McDonald shouted. "We want to see The Museum of Questionable Medical Devices!"

"Bridge, you're making a scene."

It wasn't exactly true that they drove all the way from California just to see the museum. But it gave

more weight to Mrs. McDonald's indignation.

"We do have a few of the devices from that museum on display in a room here," the lady said apologetically. "But that's all."

"This is not right!" Mrs. McDonald shouted. "The Museum of Questionable Medical Devices was in the guidebook!"

"You must have an old guidebook, ma'am."

"I'm going to talk to the manager!" Mrs. McDonald said, and then she stormed off in a huff.

"Well, *that* was embarrassing," Coke said to his sister after their mother was gone.

"Do museums even *have* managers?" asked Pep.

While Mrs. McDonald was looking for a place to lodge a complaint, Dr. McDonald went to sit down on a bench. The twins wandered around the lobby. Lining the wall was a rack filled with maps and dozens of sightseeing brochures. The twins strolled over to look at them.

There were colorful brochures advertising other nearby museums, amusement parks, theme restaurants, underground caves, and stores selling everything from Christmas ornaments to gourmet popcorn.

Suddenly, Pep gasped and sank to her knees.

"What is it?" Coke asked, putting an arm around

his sister. "Are you okay? Do you need some water or something?"

She just pointed at the bottom of the rack. Coke bent down to see the brochure she was pointing at. It looked like this.

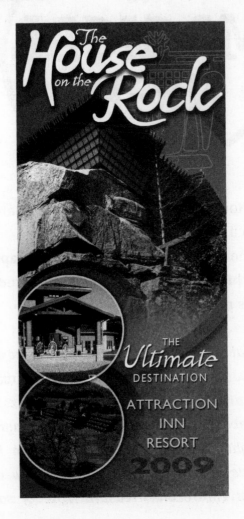

Chapter 22
A MAGICAL NIGHT

The House on the Rock! There actually *was* such a place! Who knew?

The brochure showed a photo of a Japanese-style house high up on top of, what else—a rock.

The twins read the first lines together.

"As glacial seas receded, they left a towering spindle of rock. . . . Then came a man filled with grand dreams and soaring visions. When Alex Jordan first climbed that rocky pinnacle, his imagination took flight. The result is the attraction known worldwide as The House on the Rock—a one-of-a-kind adventure and treasure trove of some of

the world's most unique architecture and eclectic collections filled with the exotic, the whimsical, and the unexpected."

Coke's first reaction was anger—at himself. If he had simply done a Google search after they'd received the first cipher, The House on the Rock would have turned up. But it had never even crossed his mind that The House on the Rock was the name of a real place, an actual destination that thousands of people visited every year. He just thought it was some regular house on a rock somewhere.

Even so, he should have known about it, he told himself. Somewhere in the deep recesses of his brain, he must have seen, heard, or read *something* about The House on the Rock.

The brochure went on to describe a sort of Willy Wonka-ish magical museum filled with gigantic sea creatures, dolls, mechanical music machines, jewels, weapons, the largest carousel in the world, and hundreds of strange objects of all kinds.

"That guy Alex Jordan who built The House on the Rock must be a piece of work," Pep said.

While they were looking over the brochure, Mrs. McDonald returned, and Dr. McDonald came over from the bench where he had been sitting.

241

"Let's blow this pop stand," their mother told the twins. "The Museum of Questionable Medical Devices closed a long time ago. I'll take the blame for this one. My guidebook was out of date."

"It's okay, Bridge," Dr. McDonald said. "It's all part of the cross-country experience."

"We found someplace even *better* where we want to go," Pep said.

"Where?"

"The House on the Rock," the twins said together, showing their parents the brochure.

"This place looks like a tourist trap," Dr. McDonald said after examining the brochure.

"We *like* tourist traps, Dad," Pep argued.

"The House on the Rock sounds way cool," Coke said. "They've got the largest carousel in the world there, Mom. You can write about it for *Amazing but True*. They've got all kinds of historical stuff, too, Dad. It will be educational. We really *have* to go."

Pep pulled out her cell phone to double-check the date. June twenty-fourth. They had to be in The Infinity Room at The House on the Rock at one o'clock the next afternoon.

"Please, please, please, please!" she pleaded. "It will be our birthday tomorrow!"

"Where *is* this place?" Dr. McDonald said grumpily.

The twins could tell he was bending.

The little map on the back of the brochure said The House on the Rock was in Spring Green, Wisconsin. The distances from a bunch of cities were listed, and it was 275 miles from Minneapolis.

"We could drive there today and visit The House on the Rock tomorrow," Pep suggested. "Like, just before one o'clock in the afternoon."

"It's still early," Mrs. McDonald said. "I suppose we might even be able to get there before it closes today."

The twins looked at each other. Today was no good. They had to be there on June twenty-fifth.

"It will take hours to see the whole place," Coke said. "It would be better to go tomorrow and get an early start."

"Yeah," Pep agreed. "Going to The House on the Rock would make a great birthday present. Please, please, please?"

Mrs. McDonald opened her laptop and went to Google Maps to see which direction Spring Green, Wisconsin, was in relation to Minneapolis/St. Paul.

"It's east of here, Ben," she said. "We could stop there on our way to Washington."

Dr. McDonald sighed.

"All right," he said. "Let's go."

"Yippee!"

243

Go to Google Maps
(http://maps.google
.com/).

Click Get Directions.

In the A box, type
Minneapolis MN.

In the B box, type
Spring Green WI.

Click Get Directions.

They headed out of Minneapolis on Interstate 94 East. There were so many other attractions in Minnesota that Mrs. McDonald would have liked to see. She really wanted to go to the town of Preston and visit Jail-House Inn, an 1869 jail that had been converted into a bed-and-breakfast. Two Minnesota towns—Rochester and Olivia—claim to have the world's largest ear of corn. She would have liked to settle the argument once and for all. But no, all the kids wanted to see was The House on the Rock.

Just twenty-five miles out of St. Paul, they crossed the Mississippi River. On the other side of the bridge was a sign . . .

Welcome to
WISCONSIN
THE BADGER STATE

"Woo-hoo!" Coke hollered. "Home of the cheese-heads! Did you know that in Wisconsin, water fountains are called bubblers?"

"Did you know that in every state of the Union you're obnoxious?" Pep replied.

Oh, it was tempting to make a bunch of stops in Wisconsin. The Hamburger Hall of Fame was in Seymour, and the Mustard Museum was in Mount Horeb. (They have five thousand different kinds of mustard from all over the world.) There was a museum devoted to spinning tops in Burlington, and one devoted to the circus in Baraboo, which was the home of Ringling Brothers. And in Neillsville, Wisconsin, they had the world's largest cheese. That may have been the toughest thing to pass up.

"Don't even think about it, Mom," Coke said. "We need to get to The House on the Rock tomorrow."

"What's the big rush to get to this place?" Dr. McDonald asked.

"We're kids, remember?" Coke replied. "We're incapable of delaying our gratification."

"We have to have everything *now*," Pep added.

"Oh yeah."

After a long drive past countless rolling hills and dairy farms, Dr. McDonald pulled into a campground a few miles outside the town of Wisconsin Dells to

stop for the night. It was about an hour from Spring Green. They would be able to get an early start in the morning and spend as much time as they liked at The House on the Rock.

There was a little store at the campground, and Mrs. McDonald stocked up on supplies. Coke did a dump at the septic tank and didn't spill a drop on anybody. The family had a leisurely dinner of hot dogs and hamburgers on the grill. Afterward, the twins toasted marshmallows and spread out a blanket on the grass to gaze up at the stars. Dr. and Mrs. McDonald sang "Happy Birthday." They kept saying how hard it was to believe that Coke and Pep were about to turn thirteen. Teenagers! Everyone reminisced and laughed over old memories.

All four of the McDonalds were in a good mood for a change. It was one of those magical nights. To the twins, everything seemed right in the world. There were no secret messages left on the windshield or lipsticked on the bathroom mirror. No evil health teachers or mysterious dudes in bowler hats creeping around and causing trouble.

The next day, of course, it might be a different story. They had a meeting with someone who wanted to see them very badly at The House on the Rock.

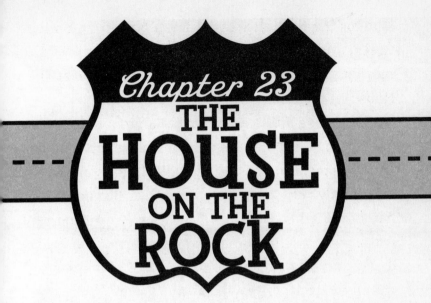

Chapter 23
THE HOUSE ON THE ROCK

There's a birthday tradition in the McDonald household: cupcakes before breakfast! With a candle in each one. It's called Backward Day. Dessert first and then the meal. Mrs. McDonald woke up before the twins so she could bake four cupcakes in the RV's little microwave oven. They may not have been as delicious as last year's, but cupcakes were cupcakes. Presents, it was agreed, would be given out at the end of the day.

The McDonalds checked out of the campground and followed Route 23 heading south through the gentle hills and dairy farms of southern Wisconsin. After about an hour, they passed this sign:

The twins looked at each other. They had lived together for thirteen years, and by now each knew what the other was thinking. They didn't have to say it out loud.

This was it. No more ciphers. No more mysteries. No more secret meetings with odd strangers. Neither of them knew what was going to happen at The House on the Rock; but whatever happened, it would be over. For all they knew, this could very well be their last birthday. Pep hugged her brother, and he hugged her back.

Coke played a mental video of everything that had

happened to them since the last day of school. The guys in golf carts with blow guns. The jump off the cliff. The fire at school. Meeting Bones and learning about The Genius Files. The ciphers. The balls of twine. Doing the dump on Mrs. Higgins. The singing sand dune. The sadistic bowler dudes. The SPAM fiasco. Dad going crazy at the Bonneville Salt Flats. Mom flipping out at the nonexistent Museum of Questionable Medical Devices. The miles and miles of highway they had traveled. The strange places they had visited.

It had been quite a trip, and they were only a little more than halfway across the country.

From the parking lot, you can barely see the house *or* the rock. Trees on all sides block the view. The twins grabbed their backpacks and followed their parents down a twisted walkway to the entrance. A group of people were waiting in line to buy tickets. Dr. McDonald paid the admission with his credit card and asked the man behind the desk where the bathrooms were located.

"How about we meet back here later?" Coke suggested to his parents.

"Okay," his mother replied. "You two stay together—and stay out of trouble, you hear? Don't touch anything."

"We won't."

When the twins were little, they'd held hands with their parents and went everywhere as a foursome. By the time they were ten, whenever they went out as a family, the kids had wanted to run up ahead. Parents walk too slowly. They have to look at *every little thing*. And it seemed like they *always* had to stop and use the bathroom. Grown-ups just can't hold it in the way kids can.

Near the entrance, there was a plaque on the wall that said a visionary architect named Alex Jordan started building The House on the Rock back in the 1940s, all by himself. It became his life's work and obsession until he died in 1989.

Coke and Pep silenced their cell phones and checked the time. It was 12:29 p.m.

"Perfect," Coke said. "We have a half an hour to find The Infinity Room. Plenty of time. Let's roll."

"Maybe we should ask for directions," his sister suggested.

"I don't want to make anyone suspicious," Coke replied. "We'll find it on our own."

Pep shook her head and mumbled one word.

"Boys."

They followed a group of tourists who were lining up outside The Gate House, which was the entryway to the main part of The House on the Rock. Once inside the door, it was hard to see. The room was illuminated mainly by colorful antique stained glass lamps. The floor and walls were lined with carpet except for some floor-to-ceiling bookshelves. The ceiling was low, and Coke bumped his head against it. Fortunately, the ceiling was carpeted, too. It gave the room a claustrophobic feel.

"This place is creepy," Pep whispered into her brother's ear.

"Just be careful," he replied. "Don't let down your guard."

In one corner of The Gate House was a group of odd-looking violins, drums, and other musical instruments. The twins—and everyone else in the room—were startled when this little orchestra spontaneously started playing chamber music for no reason . . . and with no human help. It appeared to be controlled not electronically, but pneumatically.

The music was slightly out of tune. It was an eerie sound, the tune unrecognizable.

The place was sort of like a museum, but sort of *not* like a museum, too. It looked more like a *Haunted* House on the Rock.

"I'm scared, Mommy," a little boy said, clinging to his mother while the strange music played.

The door at the end of The Gate House opened to the outside, where a red-carpeted ramp extended mazelike to The House on the Rock itself. Inside were more dimly lit rooms filled with lamps topped by fancy multicolored stained glass shades. There was also a stained glass door that had been turned on its side and made into a coffee table.

"Alex Jordan sure loved stained glass," Coke told his sister.

Judging by the rest of the house, Jordan also loved odd sculptures, big bells lined up in a row, mysterious electrical equipment, machinery of all kinds, wind chimes, water wheels, and lots of other random things that had been mixed and matched into a gigantic whirlwind of *stuff*. There was another automatic music machine, this one playing the theme from *The Godfather*.

It looked like the storage room of a museum that had too many artifacts to display at once. The twins dashed from one room to the next looking for The Infinity Room and wondering what could possibly be next.

"This place looks like Disneyland on drugs," Coke commented.

"There's something in every nook and cranny," his sister said.

"What's a cranny?" Coke asked. "I always wondered what the difference between a nook and a cranny was."

"You mean there's something that you admit you don't know?"

They had walked through every room in the house, except The Infinity Room.

But Alex Jordan's house itself, they discovered, was only the *beginning* of this thing called The House on the Rock. After exiting the main house, they saw signs pointing to a path that led back down a ramp, past a garden plaza area, to another building marked THE MILL HOUSE.

"I hate to say this," Pep said as they walked down the ramp to The Mill House, "but I have a feeling that somebody's following us."

"*Lots* of people are following us," Coke replied. "This place is crawling with tourists."

But in fact, Pep was right, as usual. Somebody *was* following them. Right outside the door to The Mill House, a tall woman with a large purse was wiping her hands with a tissue.

"Mrs. Higgins!" Pep exclaimed, stopping in her tracks not five feet from the health teacher.

The twins had not seen Mrs. Higgins since they'd dumped the contents of their family's RV's bathroom on her head a few days earlier in Darwin, Minnesota. Coke gripped his sister's hand tightly. His instinct was to bolt, but he was thrown off because his health teacher had a big smile on her face.

"Well, if it isn't the McDonald twins!" Mrs. Higgins said sweetly. "What a lovely coincidence!"

Pep was taken aback too. It wasn't like Mrs. Higgins to be charming. Pep didn't quite know what to make of it.

"Fancy meeting *you* here," she said.

"Small world," Mrs. Higgins replied. "Wasn't it *horrible* what happened to the school? Who could have done such a terrible thing?"

"Yes, horrible."

Pep could hardly believe that she was making small talk with a woman who had tried to kill them. *Maybe I had it all wrong,* Pep thought. *Maybe it really was a coincidence that Mrs. Higgins happened to be at The House on the Rock today. Maybe she didn't set that fire at school and trap us in the detention room. Maybe she wasn't trying to do a suicide attack at the ball of twine. And maybe she didn't even know we were the ones who dropped five days' worth of human waste on her head while she was seat-belted in her car. Maybe it was all a big mistake. A case of mistaken identity.*

Mrs. Higgins was carrying a purse, but she didn't appear to have any kind of weapon on her. It was probably full of hand sanitizer and disinfectant. She seemed harmless.

But suddenly the expression on her face darkened.

"C'mere, you two!" she barked, reaching out to grab their arms.

"Run!" Coke yelled to his sister. He karate-chopped Mrs. Higgins's hand away and took off.

Pep pushed open the door to The Mill House and shoved her way past a group of fifteen Japanese tourists. Right behind her, Coke knocked down an elderly man as they dashed through a gigantic room stuffed to the rafters with antique dolls, African masks, toy trains, and miniature hot-air balloons. They rushed past an entire wall filled with old mechanical piggy banks and another one with colored glass bottles, vases, and paperweights. The twins followed the path and ran up a spiral staircase to a room with more stained glass, bronze statues, and a huge fireplace.

They didn't take the time to look at any of that stuff. They were running for their lives.

As he ran, Coke turned around to catch a glimpse of Mrs. Higgins rudely pushing her way through the crowd of Japanese tourists. She had pulled something out of her purse and was holding it in front of her, but he couldn't tell what it was.

"I think she has a knife!" Pep said.

"Follow me!" he told his sister, pulling her into the next room, marked STREETS OF YESTERDAY.

With Mrs. Higgins gaining on them, the twins hurried through a replica of a small-town American street from the 1880s. There was a toy store, a barber's shop, sheriff's office, and fire station, the windows of all the buildings filled with antique treasures of the period. The trees were made of cement. The "street" was made of bricks and was illuminated by dim gas lamps. It was like a trip back in time to the days before strip malls and fast food.

At the end of the "street" they rushed past The Gladiator Calliope, a mechanical music machine that looked like a marching band on a steamboat. Foot-high statues were playing cymbals and snare drums. Dixieland music filled the air.

"You brats won't get away *this* time!" Mrs. Higgins shouted at them.

The twins were out of breath already but didn't dare slow down. There was a clump of people in front of them taking pictures of the displays with disposable cameras.

"Excuse me! Excuse me!" Coke said as he elbowed past them. "Coming through! Sorry! Bathroom emergency!"

"We can't just keep running!" Pep said breathlessly. "We've got to do something to stop her!"

"I know," Coke replied as they left Streets of Yesterday and entered another room called The Heritage of the Sea. "Grab one of those balls of twine out of my backpack, will you?"

"You're gonna throw a ball of *twine* at her?" Pep said, trying to keep moving and unzip Coke's backpack at the same time.

"No, you dope," Coke told her. "You'll see."

The cavernous room was dominated by a statue of a gigantic, whalelike sea creature that was as long as the Statue of Liberty is high. It had two rows of sharp, triangular teeth, and a full-size rowboat in its mouth. The sea creature appeared to be fighting with an octopus. Down below, a mechanical music machine was playing a fractured version of the old Beatles song "Octopus's Garden."

It was like being chased through somebody's hallucination.

Pep handed her brother a ball of twine and zipped up his backpack again. Without slowing down, Coke ripped the paper ring off the ball and unrolled three or four feet of twine.

A few people were clumped around the teeth of the sea creature, gawking and taking pictures. Coke maneuvered past them and went down the ramp to the other end of the room where there were no tourists. He found a spot where he could hide behind a beam on one side of the narrow walkway and Pep could hide on the other side.

"Take this end," he instructed his sister, holding

out the end of the twine. "Wrap it around your hand tightly."

He stretched the twine across the walkway and ducked behind the beam on the other side. The click of rushing shoes on the catwalk was getting closer. *It had better be Mrs. Higgins,* Coke thought. He didn't want to hurt a stranger.

"Hold it taut," he whispered to his sister.

Mrs. Higgins was running down the ramp, trying desperately to catch up with the pesky McDonald twins.

This room, like all the rooms in The House on the Rock, was dimly lit. It was impossible to see the line of twine the twins were holding across the walkway at about neck level.

"Agggggggggggggggggg!" Mrs. Higgins gurgled when she hit the line at full speed.

She crumpled to the ground as if she had run into a wall.

"That oughta hold her for a while," Coke said, tossing aside the ball of twine.

"Let's get out of here," his sister said.

The exit for Heritage of the Sea led directly into another enormous room called Tribute to Nostalgia. It was filled with old cars, stagecoaches, horse-drawn hearses, hot-air balloons, and some other mysterious vehicles.

259

As they walked briskly, Pep pulled out her cell phone to check the time. It was 12:46.

"Look," she said, "let's just forget about The Infinity Room. Mrs. Higgins only lured us here to try and kill us. We stopped her. I say we go find Mom and Dad and get out of here. Try to forget this whole thing."

"I'm with you," Coke said. "Gimme my deck of cards, will you? I need something to calm myself down."

Finding your way out of The House on the Rock is no easy task. First the twins had to wend their way around Music of Yesterday, a series of rooms filled with increasingly elaborate mechanical music machines. With Mrs. Higgins incapacitated (and almost decapitated), the twins paused for just a moment to take a look at the eerie orchestras of harps, cellos, violins, and pianos playing Latin tangos and "Dance of the Sugar Plum Fairy" with animated statues that stood in for human musicians. They were beautifully restored machines, marvels of art and technology. The twins let down their guard a bit to enjoy the sights and sounds.

In the corner of what was called The Red Room were two full-size mannequins standing stiffly inside suits of Gothic armor. One of them had a mustache.

"Check this out," Pep told her brother. "They're so lifelike."

Coke came over for a look.

"These guys look familiar," he said, "almost like I might have met them before."

When Coke reached up to touch a bruise on its face, the mannequin suddenly put up its arms and grabbed him roughly by the neck. The other one grabbed Pep, and she screamed.

"Don't waste your breath, sweetheart," he said. "They'll just think it's part of the display."

"It's *them*!" Coke said, struggling to get free. "The bowler dudes! Both of them!"

"Very good! That wasn't very nice what you did to me at the SPAM Museum," the mustachioed bowler dude told Pep.

"Don't you know you should respect your elders?" said the other one.

"Not when they're trying to kill me," Pep muttered. She could not break free from the man's iron grip.

"We've toyed with you troublemakers long enough," the mustachioed bowler dude said. "Now you're coming with us. Let's go. March!"

Each bowler dude marched a McDonald twin down a hallway and through an exhibit titled Spirit of Aviation. Biplanes, stunt planes, and dozens of vintage

model planes dangled overhead. Coke looked for an escape route.

"Where are you taking us?" Pep asked. Her neck was sore from the bowler dude's grip.

"You'll see."

They dragged the twins through the hallway into a room filled by a gigantic, spinning carousel. It was like looking at a kaleidoscope: more than 20,000 lights, 182 chandeliers, and 18 rows of hand-carved centaurs, mermaids, dragons, unicorns, water buffaloes, dolphins, and peacocks. But no horses. Had there been time to look, they would have seen more than 200 horse figures hanging from the walls.

The bowler dudes pulled the twins through a red tunnel into yet another room, this one with giant pipe organ consoles, a tree filled with steel drums, and a diesel engine with a propeller the size of a grown man.

"Leave us *alone!*" Pep shouted. She was trying to stamp on the foot of the bowler dude who was holding her. "What do you have against us? We didn't do anything!"

"Shut up!" bowler dude replied, tightening his grip on her. "We'll be there soon."

I'm going to die, Pep thought. *I'm going to die on my birthday. This can't be happening.*

The two men marched the twins over a series of rooms, bridges, and catwalks into a room with two spinning carousels that were filled with antique dolls. Five hundred of them, with large eyes staring intently straight ahead, like corpses. Why are dolls so creepy? Pep closed her eyes to avoid looking at them. Coke tried all his karate moves, but the bowler dude's suit of armor made it impossible to deliver a blow that would do any damage.

And finally, after what felt like a lifetime, the twins were dragged down a hallway and into a more open area. The contrast of bright sunlight hurt their eyes. All they could make out was a large sign:

"Good-bye."

"And good luck," the bowler dudes said as they

threw Coke and Pep to the ground.

The twins turned around, and the bowler dudes were gone. The large door through which they'd left closed with a clunk. Coke remembered the sound of the detention room door locking at school. That was just before the school burned to the ground.

Coke and Pep turned around and stood up. Their eyes were adjusting to the light.

It was a long, thin, empty room that stretched to . . . infinity. The walls were made of hundreds of small windows, looking out onto trees below. There was a large transparent box on the floor about three quarters of the way down.

"It would be cool to play Frisbee in here," Coke noted.

The door behind them clicked open, and the twins wheeled around to see two people stumbling into the room, their hands behind their backs. Their faces were familiar.

"Bones!" shouted Coke.

"Mya!" shouted Pep.

Bones and Mya didn't speak, and they didn't step forward to embrace them.

"Are you here to rescue us?" Coke asked.

"I'm afraid not," Bones replied. "Not this time."

"Why?" Pep asked. "We thought . . ."

It was only then that she noticed that Bones and Mya had thick ropes tied around their ankles. Their hands were tied behind their backs. Bones nodded his head to indicate to the twins that they should turn around.

When they did, they saw that a man was standing in front of the glass box at the other end of The Infinity Room. Dressed in a loose-fitting brown suit and an old-time hat, he was thin, stooped, and squinty eyed. He walked toward them slowly. A cigarette dangled from his fingers.

"Well, if it isn't the famous McDonald twins," he said. "It's so nice to finally meet you in the flesh, so to speak. And right on time, too. One o'clock exactly. I so appreciate punctuality."

"Who are you?" Coke asked.

"My name," the man said, "is Dr. Herman Warsaw."

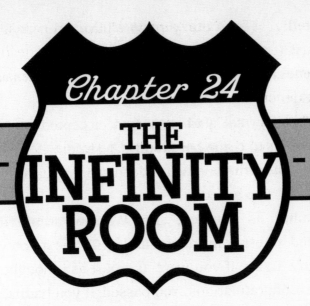

Chapter 24
THE INFINITY ROOM

The twins stood frozen for a moment. Finally, after all they had heard about this man, they were face-to-face with the genius behind The Genius Files.

"Are you *really* Dr. Warsaw?" Pep asked hesitantly.

"Would you like to see my driver's license, Pepsi?" he said, a smile curving the ends of his lips up.

"It's *him*," Bones said. "Believe me, it's him."

"I almost thought you were, like, a fictional character or something," Coke said.

"Aren't we all, Coke?" Dr. Warsaw replied. "Ultimately, who's to say what's real or imaginary?"

"Thank God you're here, Dr. Warsaw!" Pep said

excitedly. "These crazy people have been trying to kill us!"

Bones and Mya groaned. Dr. Warsaw let out a small chuckle.

"Yes. I'm so glad you two accepted my, uh, *invitations* to come here today," he said.

"So *you're* the one who's been sending us all those ciphers?" Pep asked.

"Guilty as charged," Dr. Warsaw admitted. "I needed to test your mental ability. To see if you were worthy. To see if you were as smart as I thought you were. Congratulations. You passed. If you hadn't, you wouldn't be here, obviously."

"He's insane!" Bones called out from behind. "He's going to kill you. He's going to kill us all!"

"We believed in you!" Mya yelled. "We believed in The Genius Files!"

"I know you did," Dr. Warsaw said sadly. "So did I."

"Why did you bring us here?" Coke demanded.

"Be patient, Coke," Dr. Warsaw said. "What's the rush? You've waited this long. What do you think of The House on the Rock? Pretty amazing place, eh? The unusual is commonplace here."

"We kind of . . . rushed through," Coke said.

Dr. Warsaw ignored the remark. He spread his arms wide.

"Alex Jordan is my hero, my role model," he told them. "This citadel of sandstone had endured millions of years of rain, wind, and glaciers when Jordan found it sixty years ago. He knew he couldn't improve upon nature, so he put a cherry on top. He took this slab of rock and turned it into a retreat where he could build his dream. And he did it almost single-handedly, carrying the stone and mortar up to the top in wicker baskets strapped to his back."

"What does that have to do with *us*?" Pep shouted. But Dr. Warsaw ignored her.

"Alex Jordan was a buildaholic. A genius. A crazy genius, maybe. But a genius nevertheless. He was a lot like us, really, don't you think, Coke?"

Dr. Warsaw took a drag on his cigarette.

"Yeah, he must have been a real genius," Coke replied. He moved his eyes up, down, left, and right without moving his head. There had to be a way out. This guy was crazier than Alex Jordan. Alex Jordan never tried to kill anyone. There was no telling what Dr. Warsaw had in mind for them.

"Let them go!" Bones shouted. "They're just kids! It's not their fault that your grand plan to save the world failed!"

"It did fail, didn't it?" mumbled Dr. Warsaw. "It

failed miserably. Now I have to start all over again. Sometimes you can't fix things. You have to replace them."

Coke tried desperately to think of a plan. With the help of Bones and Mya, the twins could overpower Dr. Warsaw, no problem. But tied up with rope, Bones and Mya were helpless. Without them, it was still two against one. Coke calculated the odds that Dr. Warsaw had some kind of a weapon in his pocket. The madman kept sticking his hand in there.

"The Infinity Room is the fourteenth—and final—room of The House on the Rock," Dr. Warsaw informed them. "Right now we're hanging in midair over the valley, like the beak of a giant bird. Just steel and glass. There are no hidden pillars, no suspension cables holding us up. The Infinity Room relies entirely on its own internal structure for support.

Quite remarkable, don't you think?"

"Quite," Coke replied, nervously fingering the deck of cards in his pocket.

I can take this guy all by myself if I have to, Coke thought. *He's frail. He would probably go down with one punch.*

While Dr. Warsaw's attention was on her brother, Pep slowly slipped her backpack off one shoulder. Maybe she could throw it at him, she figured, and distract him for a few seconds while Coke did the Ace Fist stuff.

"Look over here," Dr. Warsaw said, beckoning the twins to follow him deeper into The Infinity Room. "Beautiful view, isn't it? On a clear day, you can see thirty miles or more."

"Don't do it!" Mya warned. "Don't do anything he tells you!"

The twins took a few tentative steps forward but stopped short of the glass box. Dr. Warsaw leaned over and removed the top of the box, placing the sheet of glass against the wall behind it. That left a large hole in the bottom of The Infinity Room. Large enough for somebody to fall through.

"That's one hundred and fifty feet straight down," Dr. Warsaw continued. "A long way to the ground. A person could get killed. Can you imagine what it would

be like to fall one hundred and fifty feet, Pepsi?"

"Yes, I *can*," she replied. It seemed like a long time ago when in fact it had only been a week.

Dr. Warsaw chuckled.

"Oh yes," he said. "You must have been pretty upset with your brother when he pushed you off that cliff."

Pep finally saw the big picture. It was Dr. Warsaw who had them chased to the edge of the cliff outside their school. It was Warsaw who arranged for them to be thrown into a pit at Sand Mountain. He was responsible for the attack at the ball of twine, and the SPAM Museum too. He was responsible for everything. He hired Mrs. Higgins and those bowler dudes to do his dirty work for him.

Pep had been working hard to hold it together, but she finally lost her composure.

"Look," she suddenly barked, "my brother and I are tired of these games. Why don't you just let us out of here so we can get on with our lives? We won't press charges against you for all you've done to us."

"Be cool, Pep," Coke cautioned his sister.

Dr. Warsaw slowly stubbed out his cigarette with his foot, and immediately took another one out of his shirt pocket and lit it with a match.

"I'm afraid I can't do that, Pepsi," he said.

"Why not?"

"Well, that would be counterproductive to my goals."

"Which are?" asked Coke.

"To kill you, of course," Dr. Warsaw explained.

Pep gulped.

"You said *goals*," Coke said. "What's your *other* goal?"

"Oh," Dr. Warsaw replied. "I'm sorry, Coke. My first goal is to kill *you*. And my second goal is to kill *her*. I meant the plural form of the word *you*. Please excuse my lapse in grammar. It was never my best subject."

"Why do you want to kill us?" Pep asked, fighting back tears. "You were the one who thought of The Genius Files! It was a *good* thing! You were the one who came up with the idea of using kids like us to solve the problems of the world!"

"I did," Dr. Warsaw replied, shaking his head sadly. "And I recruited some fine people to help me carry out the plan."

He gestured toward Mya and Bones.

"So why—," Pep began.

"Because he's crazy!" Mya yelled. "After what he experienced on 9/11, he went crazy!"

"Hush, Mya," Dr. Warsaw said. "In theory The Genius Files made perfect sense. But I didn't really know much about children at the time. Never had

273

kids of my own. I always wanted to get married and start a family. Never found the right woman, I guess."

"Gee, I wonder why," Coke said sarcastically.

"That was the flaw in my plan," Dr. Warsaw continued. "Children don't always do what you tell them to do. Some of the young geniuses I selected didn't follow my instructions. Some betrayed me. The Genius Files experiment was going horribly wrong. I was forced to kill the program. And in order to kill the program, I have to kill the young geniuses. So I have to kill *you*. That's *you* in the plural sense of the word. I'm terribly sorry."

Pep broke down and started sobbing.

"That's another reason why I don't understand kids," Dr. Warsaw said. "They cry. Pepsi, I assure you, this is nothing personal. It's for the good of America that I kill off the program completely, you understand. Dying is patriotic."

"So now we know why Mrs. Higgins and those bowler dudes have been chasing us across the country," Coke said angrily.

"Bowler dudes?" Dr. Warsaw said, grinning. "Is that what you call them? I like that. They are two of my best men. But they proved to be incompetent. That's the problem with delegating responsibility. You just can't get good help. And you two children have proven to be surprisingly hard to eliminate. You deserve credit for that. I suppose that if one wants something done right, one just has to do it oneself. That's a valuable life lesson that I regret you two will not be able to take advantage of."

"You're a mass murderer!" Coke yelled. "How many kids have you killed?"

"Oh, one loses count," Dr. Warsaw replied. "Some are dead, some are missing, some I haven't taken care of yet. . . ."

"Mom! Dad!" Pep screamed. "Security! Help!"

"Don't bother, Pepsi," Dr. Warsaw said. "Alex Jordan designed The Infinity Room to be soundproof. I rented it for the afternoon. I told them it was for a . . . birthday party. Oh, by the way, happy birthday!"

"What did we ever do to *you*?" Pep said through her tears. "We never even *met* you before."

"That's true," he replied. "I'm glad that we did finally have the chance to meet before your unfortunate passing."

"You're nuts, you know that?" Coke hollered, pointing his finger at Dr. Warsaw. "You've got post-traumatic stress syndrome or something. Watching that plane hit the Pentagon on 9/11 drove you crazy."

"Crazy? Nuts?" Dr. Warsaw said, puzzled. "Sometimes it's a thin line between eccentricity and

insanity, Coke. Aren't we *all* a little nuts, in varying degrees? I mean, your mother traveled halfway across the United States to look at a ball of twine. And then she went to look at *another* one. Maybe your mother is nuts."

"Leave my mother out of this!" Coke yelled.

"How did you know that about our mother?" Pepsi demanded.

"Oh, I know so much about you kids. That computer chip in your scalp was my design, you know. I've been monitoring you two ever since you got them. I knew where you were at all times. I heard your every conversation. The bones of the skull make an excellent conductor of sound."

Dr. Warsaw stubbed out his cigarette and took another one from his shirt pocket. As he reached into his jacket for matches, Coke decided he couldn't wait a moment longer. This might be his only chance. Both of Dr. Warsaw's hands were occupied. He wouldn't be able to use a weapon even if he had one. Coke charged at him, ready to strangle him if necessary.

"Coke, don't!" Mya shouted.

Dr. Warsaw quickly dropped the cigarette, reached into his pants pocket, and pulled out a little device that looked like an iPod. He pointed it at Coke— coming at him fast—and pushed a button.

"Owwwwwwwwwwwwwww!" Coke screamed, falling to the floor and holding his head. Pep rushed over and knelt down to comfort her brother.

"What did you do to him?" she demanded.

"Oh, you'll like this, Pepsi," Dr. Warsaw said. "Your generation loves portable technology, don't you? You all have your cute little iPods and iPads and cell phones and cameras."

"What *is* that thing?" Coke said, still grimacing with pain.

"The computer chip in your scalp is more than just a tracking device," Dr. Warsaw said. "It can also deliver powerful electric shocks to your brain. I call it iJolt. See?"

"Owwwwwwwwwwwwwww!"

This time it was Pep who crumpled to the floor.

"Leave them alone!" shouted Bones helplessly. "If you want to hurt somebody, hurt me!"

Dr. Warsaw ignored him.

"I spent my entire life savings on the research and development of the iJolt," he said, clearly proud. "This is *my* House on the

Rock. My life's work. My obsession. It's a customized iPod. See the wheel? Instead of increasing the volume, it increases the voltage. Clever, eh?"

"What'll they think of next?" Coke said, rubbing his head.

"Before you know it, they'll be selling these things at Wal-Mart," Dr. Warsaw said. "I'll make a killing. It's a killer app! Get it?"

He broke into a cackling laugh, but none of the others in the room appreciated the humor.

"So, that's it, huh?" Coke said, helping his sister to her feet. "You're going to kill us with electric shocks."

"I would rather not," Dr. Warsaw told him. "Short-circuiting one's brain with electricity is . . . such a waste of energy. And we're all trying to be green these days, aren't we? Come over here, please. I'll show you how you're going to die."

He went over to the glass box and looked down through it at the trees below.

"You expect us to just get in that hole and fall to our deaths?" Coke said. "Now I *know* you're crazy."

"Forget it," Pep said. "We're not getting in there."

"The iJolt will kill you for sure," Dr. Warsaw told them. "But if you go through this hole voluntarily, maybe you'll get lucky. Maybe you'll hit the branch of a tree and survive. You take your chances. It's your choice, of course. And I'm pro-choice all the way."

"We're not coming over there," Pep said defiantly.

"Have it your way," Dr. Warsaw said, holding up the iJolt. "This is going to hurt me almost as much as it hurts you."

"Owwwwwwwwwwwwww!" Pep screamed, dropping to her knees and covering her head.

Suddenly, Coke came up with a crazy idea. It was a long shot, but sometimes you've got to play a long shot.

"Wait!" he yelled. "Before you push that button again, may I ask you one question?"

"By all means."

"Did you ever play a game called 52 Pickup?"

"I can't say that I have," Dr. Warsaw replied.

Coke took his deck of cards out of his pocket and squeezed it, flipping the entire deck up in the air.

While Dr. Warsaw was momentarily distracted, Pep reached into her backpack and grabbed the Frisbee. Without hesitation, she brought it back and flung it hard at Dr. Warsaw, striking him on the wrist. The iJolt dropped to the floor.

Coke dove for it, but Dr. Warsaw kicked it behind him, near the glass box.

"Get him!" Bones and Mya yelled.

While Coke crawled after the iJolt, Pep jumped on Dr.

Warsaw's back and started hitting him with her fists. He spun around and threw her off. She hit the floor hard. But by that time Coke had his hand on the iJolt.

"Give that back to me!"

"Aha!" Coke said, waving the little device around, a wide smile on his face. "What now, Dr. Warsaw?"

"Okay, if you give that back to me, I will let you go," Dr. Warsaw said, gasping for breath. "I promise. And I won't press charges against you for assault and battery. That is a good deal. You should take advantage of my kind offer."

"You say you spent your whole life savings on this?" Coke said, waving the iJolt in front of him as if he was playing ball with a dog. "Well, come and get it."

As Dr. Warsaw came toward him with his hand outstretched, Coke flipped the iJolt underhand to his sister. Pep thought about continuing the game of keep-away but instead decided on a simpler strategy—she slam-dunked the iJolt into the glass box.

"Oops, I dropped it!" Pep said.

"No!" Dr. Warsaw screamed, leaning over to look through the hole in the bottom of the glass box and watch his iJolt fall to the ground far below. "That's my only prototype!"

"Aw, gee, too bad!" Coke said.

You might think that Coke would have felt a twinge

of sympathy for the pathetic inventor, who was leaning over the glass box and watching his life's work smash onto the rocks below. You might think that Coke would have understood how witnessing the attack on the Pentagon could have driven Dr. Warsaw insane. You might think Coke would have felt sorry for a mentally ill man who, some would argue, was not morally responsible for his actions.

Well, he didn't. Boys don't have feelings, remember?

There was no time to think about feelings, anyway. It was time to *do something*. Coke spun around and did the only karate kick he knew.

"Meet the Inflictor!" he hollered.

His foot struck Dr. Warsaw on the backside and pushed him forward, causing the unsteady man to lose his balance and tumble, face-first, into the floorless glass box. Dr. Warsaw reached out and tried to grab an edge of the glass as he went through it, but it was no use.

"Ahhhhhhhhhhhhhhhhhh!"

Coke and Pep rushed over in time to watch him plummet. They lost sight of him as he fell through the trees.

A person doesn't fall from that height and just walk away.

For a long moment neither of the twins said a word. There was nothing to say. They had, in all likelihood, killed a man. They may have had every reason in the world to do it, but they had done it; and they would have to live with that fact for the rest of their lives. Silently, they untied Bones and Mya. The four of them did a group hug and said good-bye.

"Let's blow this pop stand," Coke finally said, taking his sister's hand.

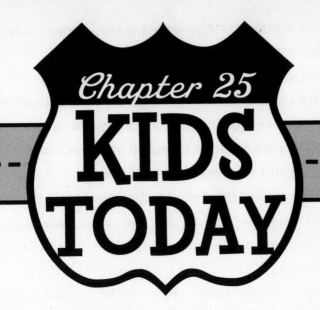

Chapter 25
KIDS TODAY

"**Y**ou were *amazing* back there!" Pep said as she and Coke made their way down the wooden ramp and out of The House on the Rock.

"You weren't bad yourself," her brother replied. "Y'know, you're getting to be pretty good with a Frisbee, Pep. I'd say you're no longer totally pathetic. You're now simply pathetic."

"Gee, thanks."

When they got out to the parking lot, there were several police cars, an ambulance, and lots of people milling around. Eventually, the twins located their parents.

"We've been looking all over for you two!" Mrs.

McDonald said. "Why didn't you answer your cell phones?"

"We silenced them," Coke said honestly.

"Are you kids all right?" asked Dr. McDonald. "We were so worried. The police told us there was some kind of a disturbance inside. A woman was found unconscious in that room with that big sea creature, and somebody fell through the floor of The Infinity Room. They had to evacuate the entire building."

"Oh man, and we missed all the excitement!" Pep complained.

"Did you get lost?" their mother asked. "Where were you?"

Pep looked at her brother.

"We were throwing the Frisbee," Coke said.

"You were throwing a Frisbee *inside* The House on the Rock?" Dr. McDonald asked, incredulous.

"Yeah," the twins said together.

"So where's the Frisbee?" asked Mrs. McDonald.

"We . . . I guess we lost it," Coke said.

"You *lost* it?"

Dr. McDonald just shook his head and wondered what was wrong with kids today. When would this generation get some common sense and become responsible, hardworking, mature individuals who care about something other than themselves? But he didn't want to make an issue of it. Not now. After all, it was the twins' birthday.

"Let's eat!" Coke suggested.

The McDonalds piled back into the RV and pulled out of the parking lot. It was almost a thousand miles to Washington D.C. They still had a long way to go.

EPILOGUE

Is Dr. Warsaw really dead? Or did he somehow survive the fall from The Infinity Room? Will the McDonalds make it to Washington in time for Aunt Judy's wedding? What strange places will they visit on the way there? Will their parents ever figure out about The Genius Files? What will become of Mya, Bones, Mrs. Higgins, and those bowler dude brothers? Are there other perils awaiting Coke and Pep as they make their way cross-country? What happened to the other young geniuses who were selected to be part of the experiment?

To find out the answers to these and many other questions, you'll just have to wait for Part II of *The Genius Files*.

Don't miss

THE GENiUS FiLES 2

NEVER SAY GENIUS

Happy birthday, Coke and Pepsi . . .

It was June 25. The McDonald family (Coke, Pep, their mom, Bridget, and dad, Dr. Benjamin McDonald) were sitting in the RV in the parking lot of The House on the Rock. Mrs. McDonald had baked a little cake in the microwave oven. Dr. McDonald stuck thirteen candles in it and lit them. That's the problem with getting older—at some point your birthday cake becomes a fire hazard.

"Can you believe we have a couple of teenagers on our hands, Ben?" asked Mrs. McDonald, shaking her head at the wonder of it all.

"Do you remember the day they were born?" he replied (as if she could ever forget). "I held each of them in my arms like a couple of footballs. I remember it like it was yesterday. And now look at them."

Coke and Pep sat in the backseat, silent. They were still stunned after what had happened to them at The House on the Rock. Just minutes earlier, they had been captured by Dr. Warsaw in The Infinity Room, a pointy extension that hung off the house like the beak of a huge bird. Dr. Warsaw had given them the choice of dying by electric shock from the wireless iJolt he had invented or plummeting one hundred fifty feet to their deaths. They chose neither. Instead, Pep knocked the iJolt out of his hands with a Frisbee and Coke used his famous Inflictor karate move to kick Dr. Warsaw out of The Infinity Room and to his virtually certain death. It would be a while before the twins would be ready to return to anything resembling normal.

"It's time for your birthday presents!" Mrs. McDonald announced.

"Yay!"

A while was over. The twins, being of short attention span (like most thirteen-year-olds), instantly forgot all about Dr. Warsaw and their ordeal at The House on the Rock.

"What did you get us?" Pep asked anxiously, clapping her hands together.

"Just a little souvenir to help you remember our fun time in Wisconsin," Dr. McDonald told them. With that, he presented them with a framed photo of The Infinity Room.

Coke gulped and Pep lurched backward in her seat involuntarily. Somebody had *died* at The Infinity Room. And it had almost been *them*. They certainly didn't need a constant reminder hanging on the wall.

"But that's not all!" said Mrs. McDonald, in her best infomercial voice.

She presented each of the twins with a little plastic bag filled with what appeared to be those Styrofoam "peanuts" that are used to pack boxes.

"What is it?" Pep asked.

"Cheese curds!" Mrs. McDonald exclaimed. "You can only get them in Wisconsin. Go ahead, taste one. When you bite into them, they squeak."

"We also got you some genuine Wisconsin cheese heads," Dr. McDonald added, pulling the big goofy yellow hats out of a bag and handing one to each twin. "Cool, huh?"

"It's awesome, Dad," Pep said semisarcastically as she put on her cheese head.

"We knew you'd like them," said Dr. McDonald.

He pulled out of the parking lot and into the first gas station on the road to fill the tank of the RV. Then he merged onto Route 14 East, heading out of Spring Green. Dr. McDonald had attended graduate school at the University of Wisconsin and knew the area well. Soon they were in the country, passing by the rolling hills and dairy farms of southern Wisconsin.

"Look, a cow!" Pep hollered.

"Big wow," Coke said. "What, you never saw a cow before?"

"Be nice to your sister," warned Dr. McDonald.

"It's Wisconsin!" Coke said. "Do you have any idea how many cows they have in Wisconsin?"

"I give up," Pep admitted. "How many?"

"One point two million," Coke said.

There was no point in arguing with him. Coke had a photographic memory. He could remember virtually anything he ever saw, touched, heard, smelled, or tasted. And one day, several years earlier, he happened to be reading the back of a milk carton that said there were one point two million cows in Wisconsin. Of course, there could be more cows now, or less. But at some point in time, there were definitely one point two million cows in Wisconsin.

"Hey, speaking of cows," Dr. McDonald said, "do you know what kind of milk comes from a forgetful cow?"

"What kind?" everybody asked.

"Milk of amnesia!"

"Lame, Dad," Coke said.

Actually, Coke thought his father's joke was minorly funny. But it's not cool to laugh at your parents' jokes, as you well know.

ABOUT THE AUTHOR

Dan Gutman has written many books for young people, such as *Honus & Me*, *The Homework Machine*, *The Million Dollar Shot*, and the My Weird School series. If you'd like to find out about Dan or his books, visit www.dangutman.com.